TITAN FIND

A novel by Christian Francis

Based on the screenplay by
William Malone & Alan Reed

Copyright © 2021 William Malone
All Rights Reserved

The characters and events in this book are fictitious. Any similarity to real persons, living, dead or undead is coincidental and not intended by the author.

No part of this book may be reproduced in any form or by any electronic or mechanical means, including information storage and retrieval systems, without permission in writing from the publisher, except by a reviewer who may quote brief passages in a review.

Encyclopocalypse Publications
www.encyclopocalypse.com

Always for you Vicky xxx
- CF

Contents

Foreword by William Malone	7
Prologue	9
Chapter One - The Darkness Rises	15
Chapter Two - The Shenandoah	29
Chapter Three - Arrival at Forseti	49
Chapter Four - Der SMS Frerichs	69
Chapter Five - The Titan Find	95
Chapter Six - The Fallen Daughter	105
Chapter Seven - Under the Influence	125
Chapter Eight - Like Lambs...	145
Chapter Nine - ... To the Slaughter	161
Chapter Ten - The Trap	177
Chapter Eleven - Detonation	191
Epilogue	209

Foreword

In 1980, I had made my first feature film, a modest effort called *Scared to Death*. While it was fairly successful, reaching number 16 on the national charts, nobody was beating down my door to offer me money to make another film. I spent the next 4 years surviving by making props and being a cameraman for Disney cable. During that time, I met a guy named Bill Dunn who was as desperate as I was to run some film though a camera. He was producer who had never made a movie before, but I knew he had the fire in him to make something happen.

Enter Moshe Diamant. Moshe was one of those crazed Israeli producers that suddenly appeared on the scene in the late 70s. Bill Dunn had met him at a party and set up a meeting. He had seen *Scared to Death*, which he liked very much and wanted me to make a movie for him like *Alien*. At that point I would have made anything. I went home, took out an outline for a space monster film I had called *The Titan Find*, loosely-based on Mario Bava's *Planet of the Vampires*. I then sat up all night doing a small concept painting for an ad campaign. I got the feeling that, more than the story I would pitch, his real interest was how to sell it. I was right. He saw the poster and said. "Beel' i want to make this mooovie. I'm goin" to make you zooo rich". Well, that didn't happen but soon we were building sets and designing monsters. And so began the long arduous task of filming Titan Find in a warehouse in Burbank.

I had talked Moshe into shooting in Widescreen Panavision. I felt the anamorphic look would give the film an epic scale and in so doing, add value in the marketplace. Filming began in the hottest summer in recent history. The days were grueling. I can still remember one of the many 14-hour days on the set. It was about three in the morning, the "stage" was blisteringly hot. I looked out on the set and saw our cinematographer, Harry Mathias. He had been standing in the middle of the planet set holding up his light meter for what seemed like eternity. I walked out to see what was going on and realized he had fallen asleep standing up. I lost 20 pounds making the film. I weighed 175 at the start. That was the way filming went.

Reception: *Titan Find* (*Creature* in the US) was very successful. It opened to mixed revues but did make it to number eight in the national charts, playing in over two thousand theaters in the US. More importantly, the film has, over time, become something of a cult classic. It's often referred to as 'the best of the Alien rip-off movies." I'm good with that. I still get many calls and fan mail on the film. I have to thank Bill Dunn, Moshe Diamant and the great cast for sticking with it. We've all been to Titan and it's a dark spooky place

William Malone
September 2021

Prologue

The gas giant hung bright in the black void of space. Its immense gaseous body provided an illusion of solidity as it basked in the glow of a faraway incandescent star; a star that pulled and dragged this giant into an eternal dance, around and around in a repeating orbit , joined by other celestial bodies that had also succumbed to the star's inescapable grasp. Each of them moving on their own set paths, doomed to forever repeat their rotation. Rotating until the day when the very star itself would release its grip, then fade to nothing as its last flame burned itself out.

Around this gas giant, immense rings encircled its equator; rings made from the remnants of ancient moons that had long since been destroyed and now existed only as icy debris, held in a fixed state, adorning the giant's hazy brown and yellow body. Like the sun's inescapable grip, this planet too held this debris around itself.

Of the dozens of moons still in one piece in the shadow of this goliath—those moons that still held their forms and were not yet part of their brethren's graveyard in the planet's rings—one stood out from all of the others. Above the shoulders of Enceladus, Calypso and Hyperion stood Titan. The largest of Saturn's moons, which differed from the others not only in size, but it was the only moon with an atmosphere made of any actual substance. The others were merely collections of gases or rocks with nothing else to them.

Unlike its parent colossus, Titan's body was solid. With its clouds, rain, rivers and seas of liquid methane and hydrocarbon, Titan was a veritable treasure trove of precious elements.

Elements which had not escaped the greedy eyes of man.

Man who had dreamed of the wonders that waited for them on Titan's surface, one and a half billion kilometers away. They theorized what might lay beneath its shroud of methane and ethane: Rains of pure diamonds? Lakes of gold? All ripe for the taking. Through their looking glasses, man had long stared enviously at Titan as they slowly stripped their own planet bare of resources.

Man's utopian ideal of discovery had always been that of the quest for knowledge. But man's reality was far from any utopia it pretended to believe in. The reality of man – especially regarding the discovery of new lands – had been, and always would be, conquest. Theft. Pillage. Subjugation. Anything and everything for the almighty dollar. The richest of them paid the poorest to get for them what they desired, and those who they paid for this, were deemed eminently expendable.

In the vastness of space, it was no different. Man, in the vacuum of the cosmos, treated space like the wild west. There were, of course, rules that man had forced upon itself, but the punishments were so far away from the crimes, man was more or less alone to do as they wished among the stars.

On other worlds, after terraforming or colonizing had taken place, any discoveries were usually for the benefit of corporation coffers. These were the same companies that masqueraded as true pioneers of the uncharted universe, instead of the machines of greed and destruction - which they were - as this truth was not something they could monetize.

Only a few centuries after Mars yielded a bounty of natural resources and riches, the business of exploring the solar system soon became commonplace. Vessels left the human planet with alarming regularity, so much so that public wonder quickly faded. The business of space exploration became as pedestrian as strip-mining a third-world country. Of course, there were dissenting voices fighting the good fight on behalf of these alien vistas, but no one really listened to them. No one really cared. And most of all, no one really policed. No one could stop a corporation's avarice a billion miles away.

Titan had been no different.

Unlike the dreams once held by man, Titan now was no longer seen as a prime destination for any excavation. The surface had long been stripped of any valuable resources, and it was quickly deemed unfit for human colonization. From then, most permits requesting passage to Titan were summarily rejected by all governments. The threat to life on a resourceless moon held no benefit to those in charge. The only exceptions made were for those who worked under the remit of *minor geological research*. Titan was considered too great a risk for anything else to be permitted. The surface was too fragile for deep mining; the threat to human life, too great. Especially when other worlds lay out in the vast reaches where even *rarer* elements waited to be harvested. So this largest moon of the ringed planet soon stood bare of any human parasites – at least officially.

As there was no real-time policing of earth's rules in

space, anyone brave or stupid enough to venture into the cosmos was free to dig deeper than had been deemed safe. Anyone could mine in areas categorized as too hazardous.

Because of this, though the black market of space harvesting may have been burgeoning, and despite the fact a vessel funded with even the bloodiest of money could launch without permission - the practice of illegal scavenging was not their purview alone. Larger corporations broke these unpoliced rules with alarming regularity, usually in competition with one another; multinational businesses doing anything and everything to win the race of commercial supremacy. And like any corporate business handled outside of the law, it would need to be done with the plausible deniability of the CEOs. Mistakes or accidents were met with unequivocal denials of entire missions. But for these corporations, this was the norm. In opposition to the laws which safeguarded human life, to the CEOs, the reward outweighed the risk. Labor was entirely expendable. Progress, though, was not. Working in space within the law was profitable, but the more clandestine work paid more for everyone. Much more.

On Titan – a moon supposedly off-limits – deep below its orange polar clouds, a vessel from Earth sat at the bottom of a deep crater.

Titan's craters had been named after the Gods of many religions; Greek, Etruscan, Celtic, but it was to this crater named for the Norse God of Justice – Forseti – that a team had been sent by the NTI Corporation on a mission of *minor geological research*, in direct competition with their German rivals, Richter Dynamics. Both companies were in a race to see who could harvest the rarest of elements first. Regulations and laws be damned.

But this *'minor geological research'* was anything but minor, and most definitely not research.

Chapter One
The Darkness Rises

"This is fuckin' fantastic!" Howard said aloud as he looked at the readings on the device in his hand. The glass visor of his space suit misted up from his excited breathing as a pulsing blue light reflected on it, filling his vision. From within the excavated opening in front of him, this otherworldly glow crawled outward, seeping into the area where he stood. Through this exposed wall, three columns made of glass plates and metal tubing framed a central column which threw out this gently strobing illumination.

Far above this underground tunnel, upon the moon's surface, a storm raged violently. The rumble of its thunder and lightning crashed in the distance, echoing threateningly down through the ground to where Howard now stood.

"There's something over here too!" an excited voice rang out over Howard's headset. "Something… Jesus, just get over here!"

Howard glanced over this shoulder at his co-worker, Peters, who was standing further down this tunnel. Peters held a drill in both hands. A portable generator stood behind him and rumbled loudly as it powered the pneumatic tool, the tip of which still thrust back and forth loudly with incredible power. Like Howard, he had been cutting into the stone wall, and, like Howard, had just now exposed something barely hidden behind a few inches of rock.

Seeing a pulsing blue light also spilling from the inside of Peters' recently removed wall, Howard smiled and said, "Looks like we're hitting motherfuckin' pay dirt!"

"Scans were spot on," Peters called back, almost disbelieving. "It was hardly hidden at all. How the hell didn't any of the other miners find this?"

"Christ knows… The CD unit says these structures are almost four hundred thousand years old." Howard turned with a grin. "What you got there anyway? I just got… I dunno…" Howard regarded his excavated section of wall. "…Machinery, I guess?"

Peters stared in awe at what he himself had uncovered. Held in large cubbyhole-like slots within the uncovered metal wall sat a collection of a dozen large glass cylinders, each one rounded at the end. Behind every one of them, the blue glow shone out through the darkened glass. "I have no goddamn idea what these are. But they're beautiful. "

Howard placed his hand-held device next to the drill by his exposed piece of wall, then walked over to Peters. His space suit felt cumbersome to move in, but like his co-worker, he was more than adept at working in it. So much so, he didn't remember what it was like to dig without a spacesuit. As he approached, Howard saw beneath the twelve-foot square of rock Peters had uncovered: the glowing cylinders. "What the hell are those?" he said in wonder.

"Looks like they're all cracked as well," Peters said as he reached out with both hands, and gently held the rounded end of one of the glass objects. Pulling it out toward him a couple of feet, the large cylinder's glass screeched against the metal cubby-hole.

"What were these things?" Howard said rhetorically, knowing full well they had no answers.

"Looks like there's something in this one," Peters said under his breath as he tipped the cylinder slightly upward, allowing the blue glow from the cubby-hole to better illuminate the inside. As he lifted it, a collection of bones and shell tumbled out through a large, cracked hole in the cylinder's underside.

Clearly taken aback at the remains that had dropped his feet, Peters urgently slid the now-empty cylinder back into its cubbyhole.

"What the—" Howard said.

Peters quickly kneeled down and said with determination to his co-worker, "We need to take some pictures."

Without requiring any more instruction, Howard grabbed the camera from a clip on his belt. He hit the large, red button on its side, and the camera powered on. He then hit the button again as he pointed it toward the fallen remnants. A photographic flash washed the area in a bright light for a second as its lens captured an image.

"Alien skeleton..." Peters said, astonished. "It's a fuckin' alien skeleton! It's a real goddamn *alien*!" He regarded the contorted remains in front of him with the wonder of a child at Christmas. "Finding a dead civilization is one thing. Finding a body… wow… Looks like it was four feet tall? Maybe? Damn if I know. A Goddamn *alien*."

Howard, with his mouth agape, proceeded to take a couple more photos, the flash of which repeated their brief but blinding illumination of the tunnel.

Peters glanced back up at the cylinders. After looking at each of them one by one, he noticed one had no obvious cracks. "That one doesn't look broken," he said quietly to himself.

A crash of lightning reverberated from the surface, causing dust to flitter from the ceiling as the ground quaked.

Howard looked at Peters. "Geez. Sounds like the storm is right above us now. We should get back. "

"Not yet. Help me get this one down," Peters said as he ignored the din above them, dragging Howard's attention back to the scene. "Looks like there's one of them intact. Glass ain't got a crack on it from what I can see. "

These two miners struggled as they pulled at the unbroken dark glass cylinder. Their initial attempt to dislodge it from its perch was harder than imagined, as something within weighed it down. On a second attempt, with more exertion, it slowly began to move.

Stopping suddenly, with the cylinder halfway out, Howard said in slight panic, "Wait a minute." He let go of the glass then stood back.

"What is it?" Peters said with a slight annoyance, taking the weight of it alone. "Help me!"

"Let's think about this... I mean," Howard said with some nervousness. "Whatever's in there, has been in there for almost a half a million years. "

"So?" Peters replied as he strained, holding the cylinder out of the wall on his own.

"So? There's obviously a fucking *alien* still in there, and *not* a skeleton, right? It's sealed. What if it's in suspended animation? What if we wake it up? It might be very fuckin' pissed and very fuckin' hungry. You've seen those films!"

Peters smirked through his straining. "Some kind of scientist you are. How the hell can it be alive after this long, huh?"

Howard had no answer and shrugged. "The glow in the walls is still on!"

"Because we connected its power again." Exasperated, Peters grimaced. "Christ's sake, Howard, stop being a little bitch. "

After a pause, where Howard just stared at the cylinders, worried, Peters continued in a gentler tone. "We *just* gotta get some pictures. It's what we're here for, right?"

"But we're not here for *that*!" Howard complained. "This ain't no tech!"

"Ain't just tech, ya know? You know what *geological research* means to NTI? You know what they expect of us? It's a *Goddamn* scavenger mission. And this is the kinda shit they'll wanna know about. It's *proof of otherworldly life*! And if *they* don't care and only want the tech here, I'm sure as shit Richter Dynamics will wanna know, and they'll pay damn handsomely for it too!"

Howard considered this for a moment, then soon realized that Peters was correct. They were here to scavenge and take *anything* of value. He *had* to think about the paycheck. Finding things like this, though not adaptable technology, would of course be of value, even a photograph. That value would be a much larger one than anything he would get on a bona fide research mission.

At first, this kind of work had made Howard feel like an officially sanctioned pirate. He loved it as he took work salvaging wrecks. But years of similar missions, over and over again, eventually took their toll. Now this kind of salvage work just made him feel uncomfortable, made him feel like he was robbing a grave. And with this alien body here, something that was *not* usually found, they *literally* were robbing graves. Despite this ill feeling, he still needed work, and if this could pay more than normal, then so be it. He had to stop being the *little bitch* Peters had accused him of being.

"Come on," Peters said, motioning to the cylinder he still held. "Let's get it out of the wall. "

Reluctantly, Howard stepped up and grabbed hold of the alien object again. As they both grappled with it, pulling it from its perch, the slick condensation on the outside of the glass caused Howard's hand to slip.

"Careful!" Peters barked. "Don't drop it!"

Regaining his grip with speed, Howard said quietly, "Hey, I... I don't like this. Not one single bit. "

Another crash of lightning above. Louder and much more aggressive than before.

As these thunderous roars erupted around them, the lighting – from both the alien and their lanterns, which lined the tunnel – all flickered. The tunnel itself shook as both men began to lower the large, heavy cylinder to the dirt.

"Don't be stupid, Howard, there's nothing not to like," Peters said, grunting as they struggled to not drop their find. "Whatever's in there's probably been dead for the last few hundred centuries. "

"Jesus, that thing was heavy," Peters gasped as they set the cylinder down. Crouching down on his haunches, he leaned over the dark glassy object and brushed the thick layer of dust from the top of it.

"Is that... ?" Peter's began to say to himself as he peered closer into the glass. His eyes narrowed as he tried to focus inside.

"Is that what?" Howard said, still nervous. "What is it?"

"I can't quite see. But it looks like a face… Kinda. "

Howard swallowed hard as he heard those words. Keeping his composure, he made himself reply, "Okay."

Peters continued to focus his attention inside the cylinder. "Wherever this thing came from, they don't seem to have been bred for their looks." Holding one hand out to Howard, he said, "Hand me a light, will ya?"

Turning, Howard quickly grabbed the small portable light from beside the whirring generator. He placed it in Peters' waiting palm.

"Jeez," Peters said as he shined the light into the dark, dirt-encrusted glass. As the beam spilled inside, it illuminated the black, ridged face of its occupant.

"It's... It's..." Before Peters could finish his thought, the storm above raged louder, causing the lights to flicker around them more violently. As they did, inside the cylinder, two alien eyes burst open with a fierce reddish glow.

"Fuck!" Peters leaped backward with a yelp, his light falling from his grasp, hitting the cylinder heavily as it fell.

"What?" Howard asked in a panic.

Steeling his nerves, Peters quickly moved back over the cylinder, then said rhetorically, "Is my imagination playing Goddamn tricks on me?"

The creature's eyes were closed.

Quickly a smile returned to Peters' face. "Jesus Christ!" he said as he regained his composure. "Swear I saw its eyes open."

"You saw what?" Howard said. "You sure?"

"This storm's playing tricks." Peters shrugged. He noticed Howard's expression grew more concerned. "What is it?"

Howard didn't answer. He just pointed to the cylinder. "I think you just cracked it."

Tuning back to the object, Peters looked down at the glass. Howard was not mistaken. A new, thin crack had appeared and spread its way across the cylinder's surface. As he ran his gloved hand gently over it, he turned to Howard. "Come here for a second."

Howard paused, staring at his co-worker. He wanted to leave, but also didn't want to create a fuss. "Why?" he eventually asked.

"Just come over here, Howard."

As Peters spoke, the lightning crashed overhead again. Both the alien and human lights flickered once more in tandem.

"I..." Howard said weakly.

"Will you just come over here?" Peters reiterated more sternly. "I need the damn camera."

Taking a few steps closer, Howard handed the camera over. Peters stood up and grabbed Howard by the arm. "Just stand here for me, will ya?"

He dragged him to the side of the cylinder. "I need you here to show the scale, okay?"

"Uhh." Howard moaned as he softly relented.

Holding the camera to his visor, Peters looked through the viewfinder. As he tried to get both his co-worker and the alien cylinder in the shot, he sighed. "I can't get you both in. Can you get a bit closer?"

"Come on, really?"

"Just sit on it or something!" Peters complained.

"You're fucking kidding me, you asshole," Howard retorted. "It's got a damn crack in it!"

Peters laughed. "Sit further down it, then!"

"Why can't I be the one taking a picture of you?" Howard knew he would not get a reply to this question. He would not win this battle. Peters always had the upper hand in their working relationship. Howard would just have to do what was asked and get it over with as quickly as possible. The glass of his helmet was starting to fog up from the flop sweat that soaked up from within his suit.

As requested, Howard moved further down the cylinder. Gently sitting on the end of it, neither he nor Peters noticed that the crack in the glass had been oozing a thin black fluid, which ran down the opposite curve of the glass.

As Howard posed, nervously stoic, Peters snapped some pictures. Each time he took a photo, the camera's flash shone bright.

"Yeah... That's good." Peters said. After a few more pictures, he lowered the camera and looked thoughtful. "Wait a minute. We need to measure it. "

Turning, he walked over to a collection of picks and other mining tools laying on the dirt floor. Retrieving a meter stick, he walked back to the cylinder and handed it to Howard – who still sat precariously on top of the leaking cylinder.

As the storm boomed outside, the lights flickered again, making Howard feel increasingly nervous.

Peters raised the camera and pointed it at his co-worker, but before another photo could be taken, Howard said pleadingly, "I really think you should sit here. I-"

Suddenly, a loud cracking noise cut into his words, stopping his thoughts dead in their tracks. The crack echoed throughout the tunnel, louder than the hum of the generator or the remnants of the storm's voice.

Howard's eyes opened wide, and he shuddered. His gaze locked with Peters'. Slowly his mouth opened as if he were about to speak.

"Howard?" Peters asked as he lowered the camera, a

look of concern on his face. "Howard? Are you ok?"

His mouth slowly opened, but no words escaped Howard's throat. His eyes looked pleadingly at his co-worker through his glass visor.

Before Peters could get closer to see what was wrong, the inside of Howard's helmet exploded with blood, brain, and bone. The gore covered the inside of the glass with the liquefied pulp that had once been Howard's head.

As Howard's body was cast down like a discarded doll, the cylinder cracked open wide, releasing a wave of the black ooze across the dirt.

Peters staggered back and screamed as the dark thing that had been held within the cylinder slowly rose from its slumber. The glass shards fell off it as it stood.

The camera dropped from Peters' hand, jamming the shutter release button upon impact, taking picture after picture of the scene. Each flash shone, paused, then lit the scene again and again.

In these flashes, the creature wailed in a strobing fury. It grabbed Howard's corpse by the leg, then dragged it away.

Within a few moments, Peters was left terrified and alone in the tunnel. Despite the monster having disappeared, Peters knew that he would not get out of this tunnel alive.

* * * * *

Glowing white and clean, reflecting the sun's rays, the NTI Corporation's R&D Satellite Station – named *Concorde* – was in a low orbital path around the bright side of Earth's moon.

With a remit of the research and development of

manufacturing processes in deep space, the crew of the Concorde were scientists. Technicians. Electricians. Not the standard type of rough and ready crew that traditionally left the confines of Earth.

Sat at a long bank of computers in the Concorde's control room, a technician in his fifties spoke into a headset as he pressed buttons on the console. Behind him, the Station's controller stood, a man of equal age who sipped a cup of coffee and stared out of the large viewing window ahead of him; a window that overlooked the moon's surface below.

A few other technicians milled about the room, going about their duties.

It was a normal day on the Concorde.

"Roger that. We've confirmed you at twenty-three, forty-five. You've got compusync. Your ETA is fifty-three, ten." The Technician paused as he hit a final button. "Roger and out," he said, ending the call.

Sighing loudly, he rubbed his brow with his thumb and forefinger. He was tired. *Very* tired. In space, time was relative. The appearance of sunlight out of the window did not mark the start of day here, nor did the moon mark the start of night. The sun was *always* here, as was the moon.

I hate that Goddamn hunk of rock, he thought on a daily basis. He was so over being up here. He was tired of seeing that same grey landscape, day in, day out.

Just as he was considering getting up to find a coffee, some movement on the video monitor in front of him caught his eye. He looked quizzical. "Sir?" he called back to the controller. "I've got somethin' that don't look right here."

"What is it?" The controller replied with a trace of boredom in his voice.

"The computer's spittin' it out at me." The technician turned to the second monitor beside him then hit a few buttons on its keyboard. "I got an approaching craft on an intersect course. It's approaching at ten zero zero zero KPS. Can you confirm it on your screen?"

With a shrug, the controller looked at his monitor, and sighed as he said, "Yup, it's there all right." Glancing up at the technician, he showed little concern. "Try to raise them. "

With a nod, the technician turned back to his monitor, hit a few buttons on his console and said into his headset, "This is Concorde, calling spacecraft approaching from Sector three. Please, identify yourself." He paused, gritting his teeth tensely, waiting for a reply.

"You are on a collision course. I repeat you are on a collision course," he said with more urgency. "Please alter your course by five degrees KW. Please respond." He paused, before reiterating with more urgency, "Please respond, spacecraft. "

The controller wasn't bored now. He was worried. "Go to red," he ordered loudly to those in the room.

As the technician hit more buttons, the controller picked up a headset from his console. "Station Control... Condition Red... repeat, Condition Red. Unidentified craft will impact in forty-five seconds." He listened attentively to the voice on the other end of the call. "Yes, sir. That's correct sir. We put the impact zone at Quadrant four, levels three through seven. "

The technician looked at the controller and, with a nod, hit another button. As he did, a pre-recorded voice spoke from the loudspeakers on every level of the station.

"Condition Red," the slightly robotic female voice said. "Seal all bulkhead doors. All crew members will vacate Quadrant four, levels three through seven immediately. This is not a drill. "

The screen in front of the technician was suddenly filled with rippling and twisting static as white noise crackled loudly.

""We got a video link with the craft, sir," The technician said loudly to the controller, who quickly strode over to look at the monitor.

Through the haze of electronic snow, a face came into view. A skeletal, blood-soaked face, with eyes fixed wide, a clenched jaw and an unchangingly soulless expression. As this face moved closer to the camera, one word slowly formed from its mouth.

"Tiii... taaaan. "

The voice cracked and gargled as it uttered both syllables.

As the controller and technician stared at the monitor, a siren wailed throughout the station. The controller placed one hand on the technician's shoulder. There was nothing they could do to stop what was about to happen.

"Brace for impact," The controller said as the technician closed his eyes.

The small unidentified spacecraft was mere seconds away from colliding at incredible speed with the outer wheel of the NTI Corporation's R&D Satellite Station – named Concorde. A collision which would surely vaporize the approaching spacecraft upon impact.

Chapter Two
The Shenandoah

Three Months Later

Against the velvet blackness of space, the Shenandoah headed on its journey toward Saturn, the gas giant that loomed large in the far distance. As a white twin-thruster *Shaman* class exploration vessel, the Shenandoah was as elegant as it was impressive.

Walking down one of the ship's brightly lit corridors, Mike Davison – the Commander of the Shenandoah – took a sip from his ever-present cup of coffee. His thirty-seven years felt to him more like eighty and change. Though young for a Commander, his years of active duty were enough to warrant him a high rank. From working in space with salvage, to scientific or rescue missions, he had done almost everything. His calm, casual, friendly demeanor and warm smile lent him an air of confident authority, which others were all too pleased to follow. *If only they knew*, he thought. Inwardly, he was rarely confident. He just knew how to fake it with ease, for the sake of others. A spooked crew was a dangerous crew, especially in space. You have to be confident to keep people from losing their minds.

Beside him, walking at the same pace, was David Perkins, the mission representative from NTI. Perkins was a tall, dark-haired man in his early forties. A corporate executive through and through. A man who wanted to be here about as much as the crew wanted him on board, and no-one was under any illusions about that. He was more at ease barking out orders from the comfort of his midtown office than going on any sort of adventurous space mission. And here on this mission, he had been doing his part to overcompensate for his lack of space experience with a bullish attitude and overconfident demeanor, much to the aggravation of the rest of the ship's crew.

"You gonna tell me?" Davison asked Perkins, as he took another slurp of his now-lukewarm coffee. "It's just all a little bit cloak and dagger, isn't it?"

"Corporate has its reasons," Perkins replied coldly. "They don't do things on a whim. "

Davison smirked as he glanced at Perkins. "So, am I gonna find out what these reasons are at any point?"

"At some point. But it will be just enough to do your job, and no more. "

Davison knew not to expect any more than that, especially from this almost professionally unhelpful man.

As they turned a corner, both men came to a stop outside the door which led to the Communication Room.

"Well, I think after three months of silence from those high up, the crew and myself are entitled to some sort of explanation sooner rather than later." Davison was doing his best to keep himself from what he really wanted to do to Perkins; punch him in his smug, secretive face.

Perkins glanced wearily at Davison and said in a monotone, "Just leave well enough alone, Commander. "

Davison hated the way this man said *Commander*. As if it were a pitiful position to attain.

Perkins continued, "You all volunteered for this mission. No one forced you. You are all getting paid whether you know now or later. So, when Corporate's ready for me to fill you in, I will let you know..." Perkins leaned closer to Davison and whispered, "We're operating under the strictest of security measures. "

Davison took a slow sip of his coffee, swallowed, then smiled at Perkins. "You've never been on a deep space mission before, have you?"

"You know I haven't, Commander." Perkins replied snidely. "What has that got to do with anything? Is that why you insist on escorting me here every time I need to contact Mission Control?"

Davison did what he did well, talk calmly whilst diffusing any tension. "Teamwork's very important on a trip like this, even if we were thrown together at the last minute. There's just a way you gotta do things to get along. As for me escorting you? I'm just being friendly, that's all. I am to all my team. Just a chance to have a little pow-wow. "

Perkins knew full well it was more than the Commander being friendly. He was sticking his nose in, trying to get information, *as always*.

"We are *not* a team," Perkins said pointedly. "If we were, I would have my own access key to this room, wouldn't I?"

Davison held out his hand to the scanner beside the door, pressed his thumb on its screen. The door lock released after silently verifying his access.

Walking inside, Perkins then said without looking back, "Just follow your orders, Commander, and everything will be fine. Maybe you will find out more after this call. Who knows?" Without another word, he shut the door behind him.

Turning away, Davison shook his head and walked

back down the corridor. After taking another sip of coffee, he said to himself, "Sure, everything'll be fine," then muttered the next words, "Famous last words. *Asshole.*"

* * * * *

Within the Communications Room, the walls were lined with banks of video monitors. Each displayed multiple areas both inside and outside the ship. Below the monitors, many control panels were littered with buttons and lights, all back-lit in purple and blue, lending this dark grey room an eerie air.

Approaching one of the main computer terminals, Perkins sat down in a chair. Reaching into his pocket, he withdrew a small cartridge and plugged it into a receptacle on the console, then leaned back and waited. The monitor in front of him flashed as it read the cartridge, then displayed lines upon lines of computer code.

When it beeped, the readout came to an end, then the monitor displayed the text;

READOUT: *PLEASE ENTER ACCESS CODE*

Leaning forward, he stabbed the eight-digit code into the keyboard with his finger.

READOUT: *YOU ARE CLEARED. THANK YOU, MR PERKINS*
PLEASE PREPARE TO RECEIVE PRE-RECORDED MESSAGE.

As the monitor cleared itself of the readouts, the NTI corporate logo flashed on screen.

Perkins smiled.

It always gave him a chill of satisfaction when he saw behind the corporate curtain; when he knew what others cried out to learn. He had lived for the last couple of months under the pretense that he knew *everything* about this mission, but in fact, he probably knew less than every member onboard the Shenandoah. That was, until now. Now was time for his briefing.

After the NTI logo faded, the monitor showed a stern-looking black man, dressed in a finely fitted, deep blue business suit. Perkins knew this man well. This was Gos Thompson, his boss and also the Mission Controller.

As Gos spoke, Perkins watched with a smile on his face.

"June the third of this year, a space probe returning from Titan collided with Concorde, the NTI space station orbiting our moon. While little serious damage was done to the Concorde itself, the probe was unfortunately annihilated, with the exception of its data recorder, which had been blown free before impact."

Nothing exciting yet, Perkins thought to himself.

Thompson continued on-screen "The stash of communications and mission updates contained in that box, if verified, could signal the most significant find in the history of scientific research."

Perkins' ears pricked up with interest.

"Six months ago, we discovered a structure under the surface of Saturn's moon, Titan. There we discovered scientific artifacts of a non-human origin."

Okay, more interesting, Perkins mused. Not the first time they'd found materials from non-human life… But who knew what they'd found? Laser guns? A warp drive? *Think of the profits in that!*

Thompson continued, "The records held in the black box suggest that the objects excavated were left there in excess of four hundred thousand years ago. NTI is, of course, extremely interested in retrieving any articles for further study."

Four hundred thousand years?

"It was learned recently that the West German firm of Richter Dynamics had been involved in corporate espionage and may have learned of this Titan find, perhaps from the crew themselves. So, their own expedition is now under-way and will arrive on Titan forty-eight hour after your touch-down. Your retrieval of these artifacts for NTI before any Richter interference is imperative and will be rewarded by substantial bonuses."

Bonuses? Perkins' smile grew larger. *Now we're talking.*

"In this file is a copy of the data discs from the probe ship and some additional information on Titan that should prove useful."

Without any parting pleasantries from the Mission Controller, the NTI logo appeared on the monitor for a brief second before the screen went black. The monitor then displayed the words:

READOUT: *CONNECTION LOST*

Perkins reached for the small cartridge in the console, removed it, then replaced it into his pocket.

Now he didn't have to pretend to know what the mission was. He *knew*. And with this he felt a warm smugness. Of course he would have to inform the crew, but until then, he could enjoy this superiority a while longer.

* * * * *

For no reason he could fathom, Davison was exhausted. Even his third cup of coffee this morning had had no effect waking him out of his sluggish stupor. He would love to have blamed it on having to speak to Perkins, but he had been like this for hours. It wasn't a lack of sleep; he'd had his usual six hours. It wasn't the mission; he had barely been back on earth for any period for over a decade. Every day was a mission day.

Probably just need another damned cup of coffee, he thought as he turned a corner leading to the crew's mess hall.

Walking out of the hall into the corridor, Dr. Susan Decker appeared with a smile. Tall and blonde, with broad shoulders, she always seemed to carry a mischievous twinkle in her eye. She looked more like she had just walked off a southern Californian beach than spent day after day in a neon-lit research lab.

She stopped and smiled at Davison, as Jon Fennell walked up from behind her. The Shenandoah's engineer, he had sandy, ruffled hair and a youthful grin from ear to ear, belying his forty-ish years.

"Hey, Susie, Jon," Davison greeted them as he took another sip from his cup. He grimaced as he realized he needed a top-up.

"Coffee on?" he asked, more as a polite formality, as he knew of any ship he commanded, coffee was *always* on.

"Should be a cup or two left, yeah," Jon replied.

"Mike," Susan said as she caught the Commander's gaze, "Are we close yet?"

Davison chuckled. "Not yet, hang in there just a bit

longer. "

"How long?" Jon asked.

"About three more hours." Davison shrugged. "Give or take. "

Susan sighed. "I don't know if I can hold it in for that long," she said in a mock-whining tone.

Davison played along as he took a step into the mess hall. "We'll pull over at the next gas station, I promise," he said.

Susan laughed aloud.

Davison then looked back to them. "Either of you know where Beth is?"

"Where else? Computer Bay," Jon replied, before changing the subject. "Any clue what we're after yet?"

"Your guess is as good as mine." Davison shrugged as he walked over to the coffee machine. He grabbed the half-full pot from its heat plate, and felt a small sense of relief.

Looking in from the corridor, Susan shook her head as she noticed him filling his cup to the brim. "You know you should cut down on that stuff, right? Can't be good for ya. "

"Yes, Doctor," Davison began as replaced the pot, then walked back into the corridor, "I have cut down. Honest." He saluted her with his newly refilled cup then walked away towards the Computer Bay. "I've been good. Only had four today. "

"That better be a joke!" Susan called out after him, but she knew it wasn't.

"Catch you later," he called back as he took a sip from his warm cup.

* * * * *

Sitting upon a table in the Computer Bay, a chess board was abandoned in mid-game. The white pieces on it greatly outnumbered the black. It would be expected by people who didn't know better that the white pieces were winning this game – and that was *exactly* what Beth Sladen intended. Her games with Davison were a welcome distraction, but that was all they were. There was no challenge for her. Sure, her commander was a fiercely intelligent man, but not in games of strategy. Or mechanics. Or computers. The three things she excelled at.

Being the mechanic and communications officer on a ship like the Shenandoah was a breeze for Beth. Everything here was top of the line. The latest tech. Reliable. Then again, if it was any different, it would probably *still* be a breeze for her. She had never seen an interstellar drive that she couldn't strip down to its component parts, then reassemble blindfolded. The same went for any computer program.

At only twenty-six years of age, Beth was the living embodiment of the half-played chess game on the table. People always assumed what was not the case. The amount of men that had told her *'let your hair down, you'd look much better'* or *'take off those glasses, stop hiding your pretty face'* just reinforced her desire to always tie her hair back and wear glasses at all times. Not Davison, though. He treated her like an equal, and for a commander, that was almost unheard of.

At the end of the computer bay, deeply engrossed in reading a dog-eared horror novel, Beth sat with her feet up on a bench. On the table next to her sat a half-eaten sandwich alongside several crumpled food wrappers. None of it was her waste, so as she wasn't the ship's maid, she wouldn't clean it up for them.

The door opposite her hissed as it slid open. She did not look up, but smiled when the person that entered greeted her warmly.

"Sladen. "

Peering over her book, Beth smiled at Davison. "Greetings and salutations, El Commandant," she said with a friendly tone, before looking back down into her book.

As Davison walked in, he passed by the chessboard on the table. Studying it for a moment, he moved the white rook then nodded to himself. He was confident that finally he would win this—

"I'll have checkmate in three moves, boss," Beth said, still within the pages of her book.

"What?" Davison exclaimed in disbelief. He looked back down at the board, studying the pieces.

"You moved the rook to E seven, right?"

He glanced back at her then turned back to the board. "How did you know that?" he asked in confusion.

"Three moves and I'll have ya beat," she said.

She enjoyed this. Sure it was always too easy, but she still enjoyed it.

"No way," he said under his breath.

She smiled and turned a page of her book. "Yes way. "

Giving the board a worried look, he then shook his head in disbelief.

"Don't worry." She peered up from her book. "After all, a commander doesn't need brains, just a good loud voice. "

He smiled, then walked over to the table in front of her.

As he noticed the book in her hands, he asked, "How many times you gonna read that same book? Must be boring the hell out of you by now!"

"Nope," she said as she continued to read. "Not one bit. "

"How good can a book called *Scared to Death* be?" he commented with a laugh.

"I happen to like it," she said. "Besides, it's the only book I brought along with me. "

"That sorta stuff's gonna rot your brain. "

Choosing to not reply, she burrowed further into the book's words.

Davison saw the wrappers and half-eaten food on the table. "I see Susan's been here," he said, as he motioned to the mess.

"Maybe." Beth looked away from the page for a second and saw the half-empty coffee cup in his hand. "You should drink less of that stuff, you know?" she said. "Bad for your health and all that. "

"Yeah, Susan said the same earlier," he said as he picked up the wrappers from the table, then threw them in a nearby trash-can.

"Well, she's a wise woman," she replied, back to reading. "Albeit a damn messy one. "

Now, slumping into a chair in front of a monitor, Davison reached for the headphones and slipped them over his ears. He needed to switch off for a while. He needed to unplug his mind and watch some mindless TV. Anything loud and dumb would do.

Pressing play on the remote control, the screen quickly sprang to life with the program *T. W. E. Presents WILDFORCE.*

As the bright images of guns and heroics flashed in

front of his eyes and the sounds of gunfire and explosions bombarded his ears, the ship started to disappear from around him. The darkness took over as his eyes closed.

Beth grabbed some headphones of her own as the commander began to snore very loudly.

* * * * *

On a monitor in the Observation Deck, a representation of Titan as a purple-colored wireframe sat to the left of the screen. To the right, the flight path of the Shenandoah blinked as a green line. The large dot at the end of this line represented the ship itself, nearly at its destination.

No one would need this monitor to tell them that, though, as anyone could plainly see from the room's large round bay window the overwhelming sight of the goliath, Saturn, as well as its satellite, Titan; both now more real and awe-inspiring than any computer image could generate.

The room's lights were switched off, but it was not dark in there. The planet and its kin provided an eerie glow which filled every inch of available space with reflected light.

At the opposite side of the room, the large metal door opened with a hiss.

Walking through, Jon stared ahead at the sight through the window.

"Whoa," was all he could say.

Almost out of habit, he checked the flightpath monitor on his way by. Not that it could tell him anything he couldn't already discern from the window. With a smile, he turned, then stepped down into the lower part of this dual-level room. This was the primary area of the Observation Deck and had half a dozen large white pillows scattered over the floor, ready for guests to recline and relax.

He walked down the path between the pillows and stood, staring out.

"Susan?" he said loudly, without turning around.

When no answer came back, he glanced over his shoulder to the door where Susan now stood, in awe. Her deep blue eyes glistened wide as they fixed on the gas giant and its moon.

"Impressive, isn't she?" Jon said.

Susan replied without taking her eyes off the worlds outside. "Which one of them is a she?"

"Take your pick." Jon turned back to the window as his voice fell to a whisper. "Both are just as beautiful as each other. "

Taking a few tentative steps further into the room, Susan's gaze did not break from the view. She barely even noticed the bank of monitors as she got to the steps down toward Jon. "I never knew this window was even here. "

Without turning, Jon replied, "Well... most of the time the shield's in place. So you probably wouldn't even notice it. "

Susan stepped down to the lower level, walked past the pillows and stood beside Jon.

"There're no words, really, are there?" she whispered. "Makes me feel so damn small. "

"Yup," he said in an equally quiet tone, before continuing, "I enjoyed looking up at the stars when I was a kid. Where I grew up in Michigan, I had this old, battered telescope. Nothing fancy, but I could sometimes see Saturn though it. It was only a dot in the sky, though. But even then... seeing this pin-prick of light in the night, I felt so insignificant. Like an ant looking up at a skyscraper." His voice trailed off as he turned and sat down on the ledge next to the window, away from the window. He took a few deep breaths to calm himself.

Susan moved closer. "What is it?" she asked. "The landing?"

"You know me," he said as he tried his best to keep his composure. "Take-offs and landings... I... hate them both, and looking out there just then... It hit me. "

"You'll be fine," she said reassuringly. "Besides, we all feel... I dunno, *funny* about this trip. We're all in the same boat. "

"You mean 'ship'." Jon corrected her with a smile.

"Hilarious," she said sarcastically without returning the smile. "You know what I mean. "

Jon turned and looked out of the window. "Yeah. It's because of *that* thing." He nodded toward the planet. "One gigantic ball of methane gas and ice. "

"It's creepy, sure," she said as her eyes drifted over the planet's surface.

"Creepy? You've been listening to the rumors from Concorde, haven't you?" Jon said, feeling better about everything after the simple act of mentioning his discomfort. "The bullshit about the flying Dutchman spaceships in the rings out there. "

"There's a lot of ghost stories about this place," she said.

"Yeah. *Stories.* "

"Maybe that's all it is, but on *this* trip – and it's the only flight I've *ever* had this feeling about – I get this," she paused as she considered the right wording. "I just feel like I'm being gradually smothered... like I'm swimming at full speed knowing there's a waterfall in front of me, and I'm doing nothing to stop myself. Like I'm willingly hurtling towards impending doom." She hesitated before continuing, "I know it's stupid. "

"It's the fear of the unknown... It's natural." He stood up and continued, "Davison or Perkins'll fill us in soon enough." As he spoke the words, he wasn't entirely sure he believed them himself. "They'd better tell us soon, anyway. "

"They'll have to. We'll be locked into our approach soon enough." Susan turned and looked deeply into Jon's eyes. "So... that doesn't give us much time now, does it?"

"Well," Jon began with a laugh, "we *are* very anxious. We both need some calming down. "

She stepped forward and wrapped her arms around his waist, pulling him gently closer.

With the mischievous twinkle large in her eyes, she turned and dragged him down to a large pillow on the floor.

He gave in to her willingly as he lay down where she guided him.

He watched her fondly as she unzipped the front of his jumpsuit, exposing his hairy chest. Leaning down, she kissed it, tenderly. After a moment, she swung one leg over him, straddling, then unzipped her own suit. Undressing to her waist, she exposed her pale skin, almost ghostly in the glow from the window.

Reaching up, he caressed her face, staring lovingly into her eyes.

He whispered, "You sure know how to make me forget about the landing, don't ya?"

"Shut up," she replied before leaning in and kissing him deeply.

From outside the Shenandoah, Saturn and Titan sat in witness to their blossoming passion.

* * * * *

Jon stood on the Command Bridge of the Shenandoah. He had still not showered or changed into a clean jumpsuit. He could literally smell the sex on himself. He just hoped that no one else could.

Some of the ship's crew were in the middle of being debriefed by Perkins, and all of them were sitting on any available chair they could find.

Davison sat in his Commander's chair, which was behind a large and complex cluster of computers. "Bad feelings are just nature's way of telling us to be careful, that's all" he said calmly to Jon, then addressed Perkins. "And I hope we're being careful here, Perkins?"

With a sigh, Perkins closed his eyes for a few seconds before speaking. "For whatever your personal reasons, and whatever misgivings or 'bad feelings' you may have, you are all merely volunteers on this journey—"

"No one's denying that," Davison said, cutting in.

Ignoring this interruption, Perkins continued, "However, this is an NTI venture and you are under obligation to them. "

As Perkins droned on, Davison saw Jon roll his eyes, and stifled a laugh. His father had been fond of referring to business executives as; *'assholes in fine linen'*, and Davison thought this described Perkins to a T.

Beth had a near-comatose smile plastered onto her face.

Wendy Oliver, the ship's doctor, and a woman of fifty, clearly resented being told what to do.

And Susan, hair still wet from a recent shower, fidgeted and shifted in her seat.

Perkins, meanwhile, carried on. "Our job here is simply to set claim to an archeological discovery. One with possible alien origin. All marked under the auspices of NTI."

"What makes it so special that we had to all come out?" Beth said. "Not the first alien stuff that's been found, right? How *alien* are we talking?"

Perkins turned to her but did not reply.

"We've found alien buildings before," Beth continued. "Kinda worthless, isn't it? Especially compared to the cost of sending us all the way out here. Must be something more than a house."

Perkins faced the rest of the crew without addressing Beth's concerns. "The find was discovered just below Titan's surface by an NTI geological research team."

Beth cut in again. "Which leads me to ask, why didn't *that* team claim it? Why are we here? Where the fuck are *they*?"

Relenting, Perkins turned to her. "*How alien* is the very reason we are here. The only survivor we know of crashed into Concorde on his return, as I am sure you have heard about. And as we cannot restore contact with anyone sent here, we are safe to assume that they all are very much dead. We are here to ensure the security of the find. Satisfied?"

Beth nodded, happy to be obviously riling him.

Perkins continued. "The knowledge of the find and its location were retrieved from the black box recorder salvaged from the wreckage at Concorde." Reaching into his pocket, he withdrew a black disc, then handed it to Davison. "These are the surface coordinates."

Wendy, lifting her fine blonde eyebrows, said, "Are we supposed to bring whatever has been found back with us? I only ask as we do not know what they found, correct?"

"No," Perkins replied. "No, we do not. "

"Theoretically," Wendy postulated, "It could be a colony of Titans, who have been living under the surface all this time. So, then what? They may have slaughtered the geologists, and now we're walking into a trap all in the name of waving a banner for a company who are still to pay us?"

"Really? That is your question?" Perkins said. "Look, we are just here to officially mark the find, then document its ownership by NTI. That's it. Not fight little green men! That's preposterous. "

Susan couldn't help but let out a laugh. Perkins glared at her.

"Okay, so no aliens then," Davison cut in, diverting Perkins' attention back to him.

Regaining his composure, Perkins glanced, annoyed, at Wendy. "Besides, if we run into any problems, Ms. Bryce has a full complement of weapons on board. "

"Where is that hard ass, anyway?" Beth asked, looking around at everyone present.

Jon interrupted before she could get her reply, asking, "Why the hell would we need weapons, anyway?"

Without looking at him, Perkins replied, "Just in case, that's why. Standard protocol. "

"In case of what?" As he asked, Jon caught Wendy's eye. "You think aliens?"

Wendy nodded in agreement. "Exactly, aliens!"

"There are always unexpected situations—" Perkins said before being interrupted yet again.

"There's something you and NTI are not telling us," Wendy complained. "There has to be a reason—"

Before she could finish, and before Perkins could lose his temper, an alarm rang loudly from Davison's console.

Turning to an overhead monitor, Davison read the words aloud that appeared on the screen. "Prepare to lock orbit!"

Pressing a button, Davison silenced the alarm, then turned to the crew, obviously grateful this meeting had been cut short. "Okay, people. We're on orbit approach. Everyone to their stations. "

The large screen at the head of the bridge then sprang to life, a bright vivid image filled the screen.

In all its majesty, there was Titan.

Chapter Three
Arrival at Forseti

"You got the EK pressure?" Jon said as he sat at his console at the far end of the bridge.

Nearer to the door, Davison sat at the master console, his hands moving expertly as he pressed buttons, flicked switches, typed in codes; all his motions fluid with utmost precision. This was something he had done hundreds of times, in dozens of different craft. Having taken him years to master, guiding the ship into land was as simple as riding a bike. "EK, Five-two-zero," he read aloud as his monitor displayed the same.

"Perfect!" Jon replied.

Davison called out to Beth, who was seated behind him. "Beth, can you get me scan confirmation on coordinates, Juliett-Oscar-Oscar-Bravo-Oscar-Oscar?"

With some surprise in her voice, Beth replied, "Shit, I got the LRV of a spacecraft down about three degrees at those coordinates. "

"Really? Get me a replay, please. "

"Aye, aye," Beth replied.

Jon stared at his monitors that were full of the real-time levels and data meters that covered every aspect of the ship's engine. "God, I love this part!" he said aloud.

"The blind panic's the best part!" Beth replied with a grin.

"Just our damn luck!" Davison chided.

Perkins, who had been sitting quietly nearby, stepped forward. "What is the problem?" he said, knowing that whilst this ascent was dangerous, there could not be any problems on this mission. Head office would not tolerate the slightest of issues. "Do we have a visual yet?"

Davison threw a few switches on his console as a monitor beside them switched its view to a video feed down into the crater laying far beneath them. This image on screen, though, was anything but clear. The thick atmosphere blanketed the surface in its entirety.

"What am I looking at?" Perkins asked with some annoyance.

"Here, I'll enhance it," Davison said as he grabbed a dial and slowly turned it, zooming the image further in as it brightened up the darker areas with a new thermal overlay.

As the image on screen became clearer and drifted into focus, Perkins sighed. "Those German sons of bitches!"

The monitor displayed the overhead view of a large space ship directly beneath them, in what was going to be their landing site.

"Can anyone confirm who it is down there?" Perkins said.

Beth studied her monitor, which now filled with a closer view of the ship below. "Seems so," she said slowly. "The specs on that ship indicate it's of Richter Dynamics design."

"They shouldn't be here yet," Perkins complained aloud. "We were supposed to have two more days!"

"Damn it, Perkins," Davison said with a rare sign of annoyance in his voice. He glared up at Perkins. "Is this your little secret? The reason this was all rushed?"

Perkins went to reply, but Davison cut him off before

he could. "You were racing us to beat Richter fucking Dynamics?" He motioned to the ship on the monitor. "Well, it looks like they won your little race."

"No, not yet..." Perkins replied gravely, "We're the only ones with the exact coordinates of the find. There are thousands of tunnels under this crater. All they probably know is the approximate location of it being within this crater, just as we did when we first sent our teams here."

Davison turned to face Perkins as he spoke slowly and seriously. "Even if we get to this Titan find before Richter does, what makes you think they're not gonna try and stop us? Huh? They ain't known for their generosity in business."

"Like lambs to the fucking slaughter," Jon interjected from across the room.

Beth added, "Think I'd prefer them to be aliens, like the Doc thought."

Perkins ignored these comments, then said to Davison, "Okay, yes they *are* here. But we know *where* they are. Let's just get us down to the surface. Okay?" He pointed to a spot on the screen at another part of the crater floor. "I want you to land right there. It's far enough to not be seen, and close enough to be able to get to the find."

Without even looking at the screen, Davison said. "We need to do a geo-scan on the surface first."

"We haven't got *time* to do that." Perkins said louder. He jabbed his finger on the screen hard. "Just punch in the coordinates and let's get down there."

Turning back to the monitor, Davison studied the image, then looked at the topographical wireframe on another screen. "I think that if the Commander of the German ship landed at *that* part in a three-hundred-foot-deep crater, he must have deemed it the most secure place to land. Just as NTI did. Now we really *should* land in the same area—"

Perkins interrupted. "Let's get one thing clear, shall we? I control this ship and it's going to go where I want it to go!" He raised his voice even louder. "You understand, or do I have to have you busted down to private?"

Jon and Beth looked at Perkins, as his bellowing caught their attention.

"Fine." Davison knew there was no point in arguing. Perkins knew nothing, but he could get them all fired from any future NTI contracts if he chose to, or alternatively Perkins could advance their careers just as easily. So, for the sake of his crew, he relented. "Sladen, punch in a landing site at four-eight-nine-echo-echo. "

With a satisfied nod, Perkins said, "See, much easier to obey, isn't it?" He then walked across the bridge and down the steps to the viewing window, itself a much smaller version of the window on the observation deck, minus the pillows. Looking out of the floor-to-ceiling window, he took in the view of Titan's surface that stretched out in front of him.

"Good," he said under his breath. "Very good. "

* * * * *

The pitch-black of the crater engulfed the Shenandoah as it began its descent downward, a short distance from the Richter Dynamics landing site.

Forseti, being the second largest impact crater on this moon, measured over one hundred and forty kilometers in diameter, and with the ship running dark to avoid detection through what appeared to be a thick sandstorm, the landing was to be slow and very steady.

The thundering of the ship's thruster engines increasingly echoed around them, the further it descended into the crater.

The flight crew sat at their stations on the bridge, focused intently on their consoles. The three of them were determined to land the ship as perfectly as possible, despite having to fly blind to an unscanned site.

Elsewhere in the ship, Dr. Wendy Oliver was sitting in the medical bay, strapped into a chair, reading happily through a medical journal. This was the one thing guaranteed to calm any of her nerves about the shaking of the ship. Science was always her security blanket of choice.

A polar opposite to the doctor, Melanie Bryce, the armed NTI security officer that accompanied David Perkins, needed no such distraction. She enjoyed the turbulence. It felt the same as going to war.

This severe-looking, muscular woman in her late thirties sat on a seat in the cargo bay on the lowest level of the ship, an ear-to-ear grin on her face.

Dr. Susan Decker was asleep on her bunk, unaware of anything except her current dreams, which replayed the earlier lovemaking in the Observation Bay with Jon.

On the bridge, Davison shouted above the noise of the engines. "FCE to auxiliary."

"One hundred down nineteen," Beth said loudly in reply.

Jon, sounding nervous, called out, "Liner red."

"Nice." Beth smiled at him.

Jon smiled back as best he could, and did a piss-poor job of hiding his panic.

Beth then turned to the Commander. "Mike, all looks good. Down one-half. "

Nodding, Davison pressed a series of buttons on his console. "Hold on to your chairs, kids. I'm gonna put you on your heads. "

"Kids?" Jon protested mockingly. "I'm older than you are, sonny!"

As Davison grabbed hold of a joystick at the far end of his console, he turned his attention to a screen ahead and eased it to the right.

The Shenandoah immediately banked to the right as it turned on its axis one hundred and eighty degrees.

Down by the viewing window, Perkins sat, strapped to a chair, gripping the sides nervously. His eyes were tightly shut as he held on for dear life.

"Hit them now, Jon," Davison called out as he slowly brought the joystick back to the upright position.

"Ten Four. Confirming ignition," Jon replied loudly. He flicked a series of switches at the top of his console. His teeth clenched tight as he reined in his nerves. Scrawled in marker pen along a strip of tape, stuck to the metal along the bottom of these switches, were the words *'last thing you can fuck up!'*

The last switch was flicked, and the noise got instantly louder as the landing thrusters kicked in, jolting the Shenandoah suddenly upward.

Jon rolled his eyes back as he let out a queasy moan, then grabbed onto the edges of his console. "Don't explode," he whispered to himself. "For the love of all that's holy, don't… fucking... explode. "

"Burn is on time?" Davison asked.

Beth replied as she read from her monitor, "Eight point two miles and dropping." She turned to Davison and continued speaking over the din. "Mike, when we started this trip you said it would be fun!"

"That I did," Davison replied as he kept his hand on the joystick, then turned a dial, all the while keeping his eyes locked on the topographical monitor.

"So," she continued, "is this supposed to be fun?"

"Ask me at the end of the mission." Davison smiled. "Thirty-three degrees, retro-engines stop," he then called out to Jon.

"Looking good," Jon replied, "Down one-half. "

"Hold on to your hats." Davison addressed the room as he tilted the joystick more to the right. "Here we go again!"

Down by the viewing window, Perkins – his hands clasped to the rim of the chair, despite having a seat strap which held him in – could not help but succumb to his fear, as a small amount of warm urine dribbled down his thigh.

With an eye on the digital altimeter in front of her, Beth read it aloud to the bridge. "Altitude thirty-three thousand, five hundred and dropping. "

"One seventy by one sixty, point eight," Jon added.

Davison turned on the joystick harder. He then reached over and pressed a couple of buttons. As he did so, they depressed and flickered yellow, joining in with the frenzy of blinking lights on his console. Blues, yellows and greens all blinked wildly. "Into the egg, forty-seven degrees," he said.

Jon confirmed, "Roger, none forward. "

The Shenandoah descended through the heavy layer of crimson cloud that lined the lower third of Forseti. Within these clouds, blue-white lightning flashed.

The expansive crater housed its own weather system, kept within the confines of its high rims. The storm it housed did not affect the rest of the surrounding moon, just as Titan's weather did not affect this crater.

As the storm's lightning flashed into the bridge window, the crew remained focused on the job at hand.

"Retro-ignition engaged," Davison said aloud as he hit another button. As it illuminated yellow, it too joined the parade of other lights.

Outside the ship, the engine's thrusters swiveled, turning their flames downward, controlling the descent against the power of the violent winds blasting into its side.

"Altitude nine thousand, five hundred feet," Beth updated as the turbulence shook the ship with a series of sudden, sharp judders. She used one of her hands to steady herself in her chair.

Jon swallowed hard, repeating a silent mantra of 'it's all gonna be alright' over and over in his mind. His attention on the job at hand, he pushed his fear as far from him as he could. He then read aloud from his monitor, "Oxidizer increased by eighty pounds. "

With engines spewing fire through the howling storm, the ship dropped through the thick and violent atmosphere. As it plummeted, lightning struck its chassis.

They traversed past the bottom layer of cloud, and the rain began to slam onto its hull. This solid rain, made of ice, battered the metal of the ship unforgivingly.

The gales that accompanied this frozen downfall were so strong the engine fought as best it could to keep to its chosen path. The crew inside the Shenandoah were locked in this battle against the elements within this crater.

Perkins was terrified as, eyes tightly shut, he tried to

imagine that he was elsewhere. Anywhere else but here. As the sweat dripped down his face, the lightning bolts exploded outside of the window, reflecting in the perspiration falling from his face.

He willed himself to regain some modicum of control, not to mention wishing to hide his fear from the crew. Pulling a handkerchief from his pocket with his shaking hand, he quickly mopped the sweat from his brow. As he started to regain a modicum of composure, the ship violently shuddered again. The ferocity was continuous and the noise deafening. This roller-coaster momentum caused another trickle of urine to escape and trace down his leg. Quickly filled with panic and shame, he closed his eyes tight, waiting for the shaking to stop, all the while convinced that the crew were laughing at him.

The fact was though, at that moment, neither Davison, Jon nor Beth had even remembered that Perkins was still in the room.

"One hundred down four," Beth exclaimed.

The ship now drifted several a few hundred feet above to the surface, as it glided effortlessly through the surrounding brutish storm. Below them, various sharp rock formations jutted sharply into the air. As they descended between them, the ice rain soon abated as the rampaging storm lessened.

On the topographical monitor in front of Davison, the dot representing the ship flashed faster the nearer they got to the intended landing area.

With one hand still on the joystick, Davison centered the approach so the flickering dot on the screen was perfectly on target.

The engines blazed away and, now less than a hundred feet from the surface, the fire within them faded, and the ship slowed its descent. As they belched their fire at the ground below, the thrusters caused the dust and ice that covered it to billow upward.

The bridge shook with the last of the turbulence. Jon, through gritted teeth, addressed the ship itself, "Come on, you beautiful bitch!"

Beth cut in. "Ladies and gentlemen, we got touchdown in… Five… Four… Three… Two…"

* * * * *

David Perkins was in his office, sitting behind his large chrome desk. The bay windows behind him overlooked the glimmering city of Nuevo Angeles; the much-improved Californian metropolis, built further inland after the old city had sunk into the sea in the latter part of the twenty-second century. He had always adored this city. Adored his life. Adored his job. Adored NTI. They stood for everything that he did: Ruthless capitalistic business at any cost. He towed the party line no matter what the command was. He'd never had any doubt.

Not until this phone call.

For the first time since he began his employment for NTI, as he replaced the handset onto the cradle on the chrome desk, he doubted his orders. He knew *someone* had to oversee the expedition to Titan. He knew the importance of such a mission. He knew the cost if they could not secure the find. Yet, he still felt like the orders were sending him away as some sort of punishment. Of course, this order showed their trust in him, but at the same time, *anyone* in a business suit could be sent across the vast expanse of space to a potentially lethal environment. Was he that expendable to them, or was he that dependable? He did not know which, and he hated confusion.

Sitting in silence, he turned in his chair to face the view of the city. He didn't want to leave, but he had no other choice. Even if he had made cogent arguments against the order, NTI were not in the habit of rethinking issued commands to its staff. Rethinking was a sign of weakness, as it would show errors in their initial consideration. If they changed one command, then all other commands could become subject to debate.

No, he was going.

He just hated that he had no other choice.

* * * * *

"Not too bad!" Jon's voice broke Perkins from his daydream.

In an instant, Perkins was stolen from the comfort of his office and slammed back into the reality of his current mission to Titan.

The engines hummed idly as the ship sat on the surface of this alien moon.

Perkins blinked the remnants of his fear away. Glancing down at his pants, he breathed a sigh of relief that his urine was not at all visible through his dark pants.

"Bring engines to a full stop." Davison said.

With a sigh of relief, Jon pressed a large, red button on his console; the cut-off switch to the engines. As the mechanical humming faded away to nothing, Jon and Beth shared a smile.

Even Perkins found cause to smile as he reached his hand onto the seat's buckle then unclasped it.

The only person not feeling this relief from the safe landing was Davison.

Instead, he looked concerned.

"Everyone please stay in your places," the commander said urgently, as he continued to read the parade of red numbers that appeared one by one along the bottom of his topographic monitor.

All relief in the room slowly evaporated. And as it did, Jon called out, "What's the matter?"

As if on cue, a low, ominous rumble vibrated through the ship from deep underneath them.

Falling quiet, the crew on the bridge all looked downward, scanning the floor; hoping that what they heard was a passing hiccup.

"Damnit," Davison muttered under his breath before hitting the talk button on the console's microphone. Raising his voice, he addressed those onboard.

Melanie Bryce's stern expression did not alter as she heard the announcement. She just held on tighter to her seat.

In the medical bay, Dr. Wendy Oliver only had time to raise her hand to her mouth in shock.

Awoken with a jolt from her sleep, Dr. Susan Decker has no time to react to the words that Davison shouted.

"We're going down! Brace yourselves!" came Davison's command over the speakers linked all over the ship.

Back on the bridge, Perkins opened his mouth to say something, but he was quickly silenced as the ship lurched backwards violently, throwing him out of his seat and sending him tumbling across the floor.

Beneath the Shenandoah, the frosted and rocky ground had cracked wide open and their landing zone was giving way. As it transformed into a gigantic maw of stone and ice, the moon consumed the Shenandoah whole.

The ship's rear landing gear was the first part to be swallowed up. The heavy gravity of this moon forced the rest to follow very quickly.

Within only a matter of seconds, they had disappeared far below the bottom of Forseti.

As the ship spun backward ninety degrees, the onboard circuits shorted, causing the lighting onboards to flicker wildly in all its quarters.

As the medical bay tipped, the cupboards along the top of the room flew open, dropping their contents outward. A blood pressure monitor tumbled across the bay and struck a screaming Dr. Wendy Oliver on her head, knocking her out on impact.

In the Cargo Bay, Melanie Bryce was out of her seat, hanging onto the open hatch leading up to the higher levels. Now, though, this hatch was on the ceiling, and the bay was below her dangling feet. Without any trace of fear, she pulled her body up through the hatch and continued climbing.

Through the permeable, cracked-open rock, the Shenandoah fell nearly two hundred feet, until it finally came to rest with an almighty crash. The rear of the ship buckled inward upon impact, as it lost the battle between it and the solid base of the cavern below.

As large chunks of rock continued to fall, the ship's natural balance forced it to right itself; the front of it pitching forward and crushing the landing gear there as it collided with the rock, ending up in a crumpled downward-dog position. Its rear, raised into the air, held up by landing gear, that – though buckled – still held the back of the ship's weight.

* * * * *

Wendy Oliver came to as she felt a hand touch her cheek.

She opened her eyes, and noticed that the lights inside the medical bay were on half-power, and no longer flickering.

As she tried to focus her bleary eyes, a throb of dull pain shot through her head, and she groaned loudly.

"Doc, you alright?" came a familiar voice.

Blinking the fogginess away from her vision, she tried to focus on her surroundings. The room was a mess of medical supplies and fallen equipment.

"Think you got hit in the head there," the familiar voice said again.

"I... I'm okay," she said, sitting upright. She turned and saw Davison crouched beside her, with a comforting smile.

"Take it slowly, Doc," he said.

Behind him, Perkins stood in the doorway, cradling his hand. "Doctor Oliver, I need a bandage immediately," he demanded.

Davison turned to him and snapped, "Can't you see she's injured? Leave her be. "

Beth, uninjured, strode past Perkins and said, "Here, let me see it. "

Taking a handkerchief from her pocket, she wrapped

it around the very minor wound on Perkins' hand.

Davison helped Wendy to her feet. "Soft landing, huh?" he said to her jokingly.

Perkins overheard, and shot an angry look at Davison. "That was a stupid move, Commander, landing at such a precarious spot. "

Beth scowled, then finished dressing Perkins' hand by pulling the securing knot with a tight yank. He winced in pain, then shook his head at her.

She shrugged with a smile as if to say, *'I'm sorry, didn't mean to. '*

Davison ignored Perkins as he watched Wendy check her head injury in the mirror.

"So what now?" Perkins asked.

Turning, Davison replied, "Now you all go back to the bridge. I gotta go to engineering. "

As if he was trying to start an argument, Perkins retorted, "I will *not* be ordered to the bridge like a low-level crew member. I will be coming *with you*. "

With a sigh, Davison nodded. He had no time to argue with this man. If he wanted to come along, fine. There were larger problems at hand.

In Susan's bunk room, Jon sat on the bed next to her, worried.

"I'm fine, really. Just a few bumps and bruises," she said with a smile.

"Guess I wasn't overreacting about the landing, huh?"

Before she could reply, the intercom on the wall sprang to life. Davison's voice sounded from the speaker. "Jon? Susan? All okay down there?"

Leaning forward, Jon pressed the talk button on the

wall. "All copasetic here. I guess any landing you can walk away from is a good one, right?"

"That remains to be seen," Davison replied. "Now, if you're up to it, Jon, I need you to run some diagnostics. Can you meet me in engineering?"

Jon looked at Susan, checking she was okay with their Commander's request.

Susan smiled and said, "He'll be there, Boss!"

* * * * *

On a lower level of the Shenandoah, Engineering had suffered no obvious technical damage from the fall. Though the room itself was now cocked at a slight angle, all the computer and console lights flashed away just as they should. It was only the cracked pipes that ran around the room, as they slowly hissed out their steam, coupled with the minor debris scattered on the floor that displayed any signs of the crash.

At one of its consoles, Davison poured himself a cup of coffee from a thermos - a thermos he had kept at his side during the ship's arrival. Now, he couldn't be more relieved that he had done so. He had not seen the mess hall, but knew that the coffee machine would in all likelihood have met with a terrible end; the effect of having fallen through the moon's surface, unsecured to its sideboard.

Standing by the door, Perkins waited for Jon to enter.

Davison smirked as it seemed to him that Perkins would feel that he *had* to be the one who took charge. Despite having no rank, he was obviously the kind of suit that believed he had unbridled authority out here. He was not the sort of man that would allow anyone, not even Davison as captain, to relegate him to a spectator status.

"Well, let's have it..." Perkins said, when Jon at last entered the room, not even allowing him a chance to breathe. "How long before we can take off?"

Jon looked at Perkins blankly, "I'd say about… never?" he said, then turned to speak to Davison instead. "We're not going to be able to fly anywhere in this thing."

Davison nodded, knowing full well what Jon was saying was indeed correct. Anyone could tell from the internal damage that the situation was dire. The captain just needed confirmation by the engineer.

Perkins was not as realistic. "What are you saying?" he said in a panic. "Are you telling me that you cannot fix this craft? That we're stuck here? Well, that's not *good enough*! You must be able to—"

With a smirk of annoyance, Jon turned to Perkins. "I *must,* doesn't mean I *can*!" he interrupted. "What I'm saying is that the ship is trashed. Totally and unequivocally *fucked*. The cooling units for the fusion accelerator are not only inoperative, but sheared from their fixings. Drive engines one, four and five got torn off the damn chassis in the fall. Not to mention that the atmosphere generator and reserve units have totally seized up."

Perkins stared at him, wide-eyed with fear.

Jon continued, "And that means, that in just a few short hours, we're going to be on bottled air, and you know what *that* means?"

Without waiting for any more, Davison walked over to the intercom on the wall. Pressing the button, he said "Sladen?"

Perkins and Jon watched silently, not knowing what

he was going to ask of Beth. Or what his plan currently was.

"Yeah, Mike, I'm here," came Beth's voice.

"I need you to hail the Richter Dynamics ship," he said, as his gaze met Perkins'.

"Okay," Beth replied, "but I don't know if we'll be able to cut through the RF interference from the storm, or through the rock above us."

"Try anyway and then see about reaching Concorde, not that I think that is possible either."

Striding over with a furious look, Perkins pushed his way past Davison to the intercom, then mashed the button hard with his thumb. "Cancel that order!" he shouted at Beth.

Glaring at Davison, Perkins said angrily, "We are *not* asking Richter Dynamics for *anything*."

With Perkins' thumb still on the intercom, Beth could hear what Davison said next. She heard the assured calm in his tone. There was no trace of anger, only authority.

"Let's get one thing straight," Davison said to Perkins. "We are now in what your corporate manual would call 'a life-threatening situation', you got that? So from now on, and according to your own company rules, your authority on this ship is severely reduced. NTI regulations clearly state that in such a situation, the commander assumes total operational control of all aspects until safety is resumed."

Beth smiled as she could hear Perkins' cowardice in the ensuing silence.

"Am I making myself clear, Mr. Perkins?" Davison asked calmly.

The intercom cut off as Perkins then backed away, intimated yet still angry. "I will make sure you are fired for this."

Instead of getting the required apology from Davison, all he got was a laugh.

"Good..." Davison said, not fazed by the threat in the slightest. "Then we don't need to have any further discussions, now do we?"

Hitting the intercom button again, Davison addressed Perkins. "Sladen? Ignore our aggravating guest. The situation has clearly made him forget my authority. Please attempt those messages immediately."

Perkins wanted to scream at this insolence. He wanted to shout the house down. Oh, how he wished the situation were different. He knew that if they were standing in his office in Nuevo Angeles, Davison would not be so cocky. In fact, he would cower and beg not to be fired.

Beth's voice came over the speaker. "I actually already tried while you were all shouting."

Davison let out a laugh as Perkins grumbled.

She continued, "But I got no response. I've got no way of even knowing if we're getting through. It's just static. And as for Concorde? Not a chance in hell. Got a better chance of calling my dead grandfather."

"Well, may as well keep trying for the German ship," Davison replied

"Yes, sir," she answered.

Davison released the button to the intercom.

"I best go dust off our EVA suits then," Jon said, as he turned to leave the room.

"What?!" Perkins said, confused.

Davison walked over. "Well, since we can't talk to

our neighbors, we better take a walk over to see if they can give us a lift home. Unless of course you think staying here to slowly suffocate would be preferable?"

Perkins had no plan to solve any of this. He just hated the thought of asking Richter Dynamics for anything. Head Office would probably fire him for this.

Jon took another step to leave, and suddenly stopped again when Bryce walked in carrying a large rifle.

Perkins saw her and smiled.

"Before anyone gets any ideas," Davison said, "those weapons better stay onboard. We're going to be asking them for help, not going into a battle. "

Perkins spoke up before Bryce could reply, her expression obviously objecting to the commander's order. "Miss Bryce here follows *my* orders, Commander... And no emergency status will change that. So, she will bring her weapons, no matter if you object or not. "

Jon looked at Davison with a shrug. "We might need them, Boss. Remember, people died up here. Ain't just Richter Dynamics we gotta be wary of…"

Chapter Four
Der SMS Frerichs

High above the wreck of the Shenandoah, the fearsome storm roared along the crater's basin. It screamed through Titan's deep red atmosphere, sending its blue-white lightning cascading downwards, through the broken surface into the newly exposed caverns. What had never seen light before now basked in the storm's flashing power.

The ship had fallen through the unstable ground, down into an immense catacomb-like cavern. Within it, lining all surfaces surrounding this downed craft, black rocks had formed over the millennia into many bizarre shapes. Shapes that resembled both thick roots of trees that had grown and interwoven around one another, as well as large Swiss-cheese-like slabs, which in the darkness looked like giant spider webs.

Crawling its way through this underground network of caverns, a fog of methane and hydrogen-cyanide gave the vista an air of added lethality. If a man were to stand here without an oxygen tank, the fog would melt their lungs within a few minutes, asphyxiating them.

* * * * *

After forty-five minutes of walking through the many underground caverns, each filled with deadly mist, the crew of the Shenandoah had traveled far away from the temporary safety of their vessel. Each of them were covered from head to toe with spacesuits made from glass, plastic and cloth. Each of these form-fitting suits were gray and carried their own embroidered name tags. The suit's flexible tubing, much like a network of veins, ran the length of their outfits, connecting not only their air supply to their helmets, but sending a liquid coolant around their body, to regulate their temperature.

Each had flashlights affixed to the front of their suits, which cast bright, narrow beams over the ground that lay in front of them.

At the head of this group, Davison walked first. In his hand, he held an electronic scanner that he rarely took his eyes off.

"Stay in sight of each other when we get up to the surface," he whispered. His voice fed via intercom into each of the other crew members' inbuilt headphones. "We won't be able to communicate if you're not close by. The interference is far too heavy."

"How the hell are we gonna find the other ship?" Susan said, as she looked downward, taking each step ahead of her as carefully as she could.

Jon, walking beside her, pointed to Davison up front. "I adjusted the topographical scanner. Now it also locks onto any radiation that comes from their ship's fusion unit."

Susan smiled, but that answer clearly did not make her feel the slightest bit better. If there was radiation elsewhere in the vicinity, then the device would not only be useless but could potentially lead them into a more deadly environment.

Coming up from the rear, Beth looked around at the

rocks. Her eyes were wide, and for the first time since embarking on this mission, she had dropped her protective veneer of aloofness. "I hope there's no geological indiscretion ahead," she said as her eyes tracked up the monolithic stone around them.

"Indiscretion?" Jon asked.

Wendy glanced over her shoulder toward Beth. "You mean like a canyon or something?"

"That, or a river of methane, or underground volcano," Beth mused. "This subterrain hasn't been charted in any of our databases." She moved up alongside Jon, then patted him on his shoulder, joking, "Nice place you've brought us to, you asshole!"

Not in a joking mood, Susan asked, "Jon, what did you say the temperature was?"

"On a warm day? 288 degrees below zero."

"Christ!" Beth exclaimed, "Thank fuck for our suits!"

"Think of it like camping," Jon said, feeling unusually calm in this dire situation.

"I'm *never* going camping with you again," Susan shot back, unintentionally making a joke. Beth laughed.

Perkins and Bryce meanwhile, walked side by side. Perkins had often let it be known that Bryce made him feel safe. Not only did she routinely carry a small arsenal of guns, but she also boasted a decade of battlefield experience.

"Up ahead," Davison called out as he looked up from the scanner in his hands.

Coming to a stop, everyone slowly looked upward at the steep rock face Davison now pointed to.

"This is where we climb," Davison said.

No one replied, which spoke volumes about their collective dread.

"Right at the top," Davison said as he clipped the scanner to his belt. "That's where their ship should be waiting for us. "

"Should be?" Perkins asked. "What do you mean, should be?"

Ignoring the question, Davison was the first to climb up onto the rocks.

Jon, noticing Susan's weary expression said, "It's okay, babe. Lots to hold onto. And I'll be right behind you the whole way. Besides, in this atmosphere, you weigh next to nothing. "

* * * * *

The rockface, though large, only took them five minutes to ascend. Much to Davison's surprise, none of his crew slipped. None of them needed any assistance; not even Perkins. The lighter gravity here helped the whole operation run smoothly.

When they had all reached the rock's summit and walked out onto the ground of the Forseti crater, they found themselves in the imposing shadow of the German spaceship, whose silhouette stood high above. Compared to the Shenandoah, this ship was a dozen times its size. It could easily house dozens more crewmen, and as Davison silently feared, many more weapons. It seemed more military than corporate in design. Sleek with edges that looked sharp from their severe chrome angles.

This craft had landed in an area cloaked within the darkness thrown down by the crater's wall. These walls themselves, despite being in the distance, still towered up above them like a mountain.

The storm itself had passed over, though its heavy

red clouds still lurked high above. As with all weather in Forseti, these storms never really ended, they just paused temporarily, giving the crater a small respite before they returned just as strong as ever.

Davison stared up at the behemoth ship. On the side of its metal dorsal fin, the Richter Dynamics logo was emblazoned in black. Beside it, a German flag, then the ship's name in large block letters; *Der SMS Frerichs.*

"Let's hope they're welcoming to visitors," Davison said, more to himself than his crew. Despite not wanting guns brought, standing here now, he was silently glad they at least had a modicum of protection.

* * * * *

"What the hell?" Jon said in shock, now standing with Davison in front of the SMS Frerichs' airlock.

Having ascended the ladder affixed to the side of this vessel, they had ventured a dozen feet up to where the airlocked entrance stood, and was now wide open. Beyond this, though, the interior door had remained closed.

"Guess they could've been expecting us?" Davison posited, but a dread feeling seeped through his guts, that this was not a welcome, but a warning.

"What is it?" Susan called from the surface below.

Turning, Jon peered over the edge to the crew standing in wait. "Door's been left open. "

Bryce slung her rifle over her shoulder, grabbed the ladder and clambered up speedily.

Davison noticed her approaching, then sighed. Though he liked her personally, she was Perkins' muscle - and as the Captain disliked that man - by process of providence, he *had* to dislike Bryce too. Purely out of principle.

Moving herself off the ladder to stand in between Jon and Davison, Bryce grabbed her weapon and leveled its sight toward the closed interior door.

Grabbing the rifle's barrel with his hand, Davison forced it downwards. "Take it easy, soldier," he said.

Cracking a small smile, she locked eyes with him. *There was no need to question his command – yet*. She quickly relaxed her aim.

"Wait," Susan called from down below, "Jon, I'm coming with you. "

Perkins shook his head at what he deemed to be folly on Susan's behalf. He had always believed that the adage of *fortune favors the bold*, should instead be *fortune favors the cautious*. Why else would any general wait far away from the battlefield as their soldiers fought? They were cautious to not put their own lives in jeopardy, so Susan's running into this midst of uncertainty, though indeed bold, also placed her square into the expendable category earned by the many nameless soldiers that died in history's battles.

As Susan joined Bryce and Jon at the airlock, Davison walked inside the hatch, then stood next to the interior door. Ushering them inward with him, he spoke over the intercom to Beth, Perkins and Wendy, who were waiting outside. "We're going in. Comms won't reach us from out here, so if we're needed, come find us… Beth, you're in charge." He didn't have to see their reaction to know that Perkins was surely fuming silently at this order.

Bryce hit the button on the inside of the hatch. With a loud hiss and a plume of smoke, the airlock door slid down from inside its frame, slamming shut with speed. The sound of a loud *clunk* rang out as it locked into place.

As soon as the lock engaged, a blast of air hit them

from all sides, and the pipes in the sealed hatch equalized the air pressure and refilled the room with oxygen.

Jon glanced at the readout on the small display screen on the wall. The numbers on it read *1. 5 bar*, and slowly dropped increment by increment until it reached *1. 0 bar*.

As it hit *1. 0*, the interior door automatically slid sideways, opening the ship to them. Dark and foreboding, the corridor was anything but welcoming. It was empty, shadow-filled and bleak.

"Once more unto the breach, dear friends," Davison said under his breath as he took a step into the body of the ship. The three behind followed him closely.

As the door shut behind them, Davison slowly twisted the ring-lock under his helmet, which hissed as the oxygen seal broke. Removing it, he took a deep breath in, then turned to the other three. "If you want to, feel free to take your helmets off; keep them with you at all times, though. "

"Don't think anyone wants to keep these on any more than they have to," Jon said, removing his helmet.

Susan quipped, "Why do you think I came with you?"

Jon nudged her gently as he replied in mock-offense, "Not for my addicting personality?"

Before she could answer, Davison called out down the corridor. "Hello, anyone here? Guten tag!"

Silence.

"You speak German?" Jon said quietly.

"Not in the slightest,' Davison smiled. "Literally just that. "

They continued cautiously, walking down the narrow passageway and through an open bulkhead door, until they came to a room next to a metal staircase leading upward. Davison led them into the room.

The room had two long chrome tables, both lining either side of the room. As they all took tentative steps forward, the team glanced at the tables where a multitude of strange and unidentifiable gadgets had been placed, as if on display. Some glowed a sickly green hue, some pulsed and ticked like a heartbeat. Blinking and flashing lights adorned many of them. These lights illuminated this dark room as if it were a surreal disco.

Behind both of these tables, adding to this flurry of illumination from the gadgets, banks of hundreds of lights spanned each wall. Each of these lights were square, two inches in size ,and flashed with an intermittent dull, white glow. Though this glow paled in compared to the brightness rising from the gadgets.

"I would say we need one of these rooms on our ship," Jon said as he watched the reflected glow of the lights on the ceiling. "But I have no clue what the hell it is. "

"Probably to do with the excavation. Maybe it's what they found out there?"

They looked around at the objects, knowing better than to get closer to them. A wide berth was the intelligent course of action when dealing with foreign tech. Especially as it might be a lot more foreign than simple German origin.

Davison turned to them. "We'd get this done quicker if everyone spreads out in groups, okay?"

Everyone nodded except Susan, who insisted, "I'm staying with Jon. "

Before any more could be said, Bryce walked ahead and out of the door, saying, "I'll go alone."

Jon shook his head and smirked at the commander. "Such a friendly lady. "

"Can you go see if you can get more power in this beast?" Davison motioned to the darkness around the room. "Seems to be running on emergency power. "

"You think the crew left?"

"No idea," Davison replied. "But it sure does seem like a damn ghost ship."

Outside of the ship, Wendy, Perkins and Beth were now standing directly by the closed airlock door, having climbed the ladder.

Beth leaned to the side of the ship next to the ladder that continued to stretch upward. She turned up the volume on her headset via the interface screen on her sleeve, hoping to hear those inside, but as Davison noted, there was nothing except static interference. With a disappointed look, she turned down the volume again.

Dr. Wendy Oliver paced back and forth across the small metal area.

Perkins stood back, barely masking his contempt for both of them.

"You better quit that, Doc," Beth said.

"What?" Wendy replied, slowing her pacing. "Stop what?"

"Walking about like that." Beth motioned to the doctor's legs. "You'll use up too much oxygen. "

Coming to a full stop, Wendy then replied under her breath, "Oh, yeah. It slipped my mind." She shook her head quickly as if casting the forgetfulness away from her, like a dog shaking water from its coat.

Perkins grimaced as he glanced at the solid airlock door. "I don't like this waiting. We should go back to the ship, not just stand here like idiots. "

Giving each other a knowing glance as if to say, *'What a jerk,'* Wendy and Beth did not reply.

Perkins continued, "They can come get *us* if they succeed. What is the point of us just standing here?"

Soon realizing that he would be on his own if he were to journey back to the crashed Shenandoah, he closed his mouth, keeping his opinions about the matter quiet.

The darkened room flooded with brightness as Davison walked in, the torch on his spacesuit lighting his way, casting enormous shadows around its narrow beam with each step.

Passing a panel on the wall, he flicked a few of the switches hopefully, praying a light would turn on.

They did not.

Nothing happened. Not even an illumination on the panel.

Jon was in a room filled with powered down machines, computers, monitors and control panels, that all looked to be without power. He scanned a section of fuses and breakers on a far wall, reading every bit of German text silently to himself. Each word he read, he mouthed, hoping their translations would ring familiar. He was determined to fully power up this metal carcass of a craft.

Leaving him to his work, Susan walked toward an open doorway on the opposite side of the room. She squinted into its darkness as her flashlight attempted to illuminate as much as it could reach.

"Looks like a medical room," she said back to Jon, who did not hear. He remained too engrossed in his problem-solving.

"Anybody here?" she called out, as she stepped into the adjacent room.

Jon glanced back over his shoulder as she took a couple steps into the darkness.

He saw, a few moments later, a large glass door close silently behind her.

Moving through what she could see now was some kind of examination room, Susan passed several large powered down computers until she came to a large, silver examining table. Her torch beam shone over the large item that lay on top of it; a broken-glassed cylinder. Over six feet long, with a wet sheen on the inside, and a strange dark slime coating the bottom.

She approached this table slowly, intent on seeing every inch of this object that she could.

Not fully aware of her surroundings, the helmet in her hand grazed a row of racked test tubes on a low shelf as she passed them by. The sound of their cracking stole her away from her investigation. Quickly disconnecting the air hose from her suit with a frustrated grunt, she placed her helmet down on the top of the shelf, grimaced at the broken glass on the floor, then resumed her approach.

Coming to a stop in front of the broken cylinder, she stared at it intently. Her flashlight illuminated its insides. Deep within, she saw more of the thick slimy substance, glistening darkly in the torch's beam. Whatever this *gloop* was, she could tell that something living would have produced it, whether plant or animal. Some*thing* excreted it. She then came to the realization that NTI had asked for a biologist on the crew. Specifically, an animal biologist.

She had initially presumed that she was here for her

old research on cloning applications within the confines of space, but here and now, she felt confident that this was *not* the reason. A coldness shuddered down her spine as she swallowed hard and thought to herself, *could this be a sarcophagus of something... other*?

A crack of glass behind her sent her spinning round, as she came face to face with a grinning Jon.

"Sonofabitch!" she gasped, then slapped him on the chest with the back of her hand.

"Sorry. I'll try to make more noise next time." As he spoke, his eyes drifted beyond her to the examination table.

His grin dropped as he tilted the flashlight on his suit toward the cylinder. "What on God's green fuck is that?"

Turning to the table, Susan replied, "I'm not sure. But from the matter inside, as well as the condensation, I think it *may* be some kind of... incubator." Moving around to the cylinder, she tapped on its glass. "It is definitely a synthetic apparatus. "

Turning to the tray beside the table, adorned with medical tools, she picked up a long scalpel. She reached into the cylinder, and used the blade of the scalpel to scoop up a small amount of the residue. Bringing her hand out, she inspected the black matter that dripped from the blade.

With her free hand, she aimed her flashlight toward the extracted specimen. Her eyes narrowed as she focused all of her attention on it. "Seems very much organic. Maybe a variation of a defense excretion of some kind? Like octopus ink?"

"So it's an alien thing? Are you fucking kidding me? An *alive* alien thing?"

Susan turned, attempting a comforting smile. "I'm

just hypothesizing. I'm an animal biologist, after all. Besides, just because there are secretions, it does not mean that whatever made it is alive at all. This could be synthesized. "

"That's all we need, one more mystery." Jon shook his head. "Anyway, we should go. Better go see if anyone has been found on this thing. And I gotta go to the bridge to switch all this on, I think." He then pointed to her helmet on the shelf. "Connect your helmet or Mike's gonna be pissed."

"You go ahead. I just wanna check a couple of things with this, okay?"

"On your own?" Jon said in surprise, "really?"

A look from her was all it took for him to relent in his questioning. She hated being treated like a child. He might be older than her, but she was more adult than he had ever been, and more than capable of being in a darkened room alone.

"I'll be up in a minute," she said as she leaned in, planting a small kiss on his lips. "Meet you on the bridge?"

"Sure." He smiled as she turned away from him, back to the table. "I'll allow it just this once," he jokingly added.

"Thanks, Dad," she replied, taking a closer look at the residue on the cylinder's glass. She did not see his silent grimace at her words. He was *nearly* old enough to be her father. And that was a thought that occasionally made him feel like a creep. He didn't need her reminding him.

The cargo bay of the SMS Frerichs was significantly larger than the one on the Shenandoah. In its half-light, the wall looked infinite as the ceiling masked itself in the shadows. High above, a metal cargo net hung suspended. Around the room was a wealth of crates and boxes, all stacked high.

Even with her flashlight brightening up the room, making it look less infinite in size, it still impressed Bryce. It was so large that if someone took the Shenandoah to pieces, she thought, they could probably fit all those pieces in here, without much effort.

Bringing her gun level in front of her, the flashlight on it affixed to where she aimed – the one on her suit being switched off as she deemed it too weak – she stepped cautiously around the crates and boxes, underneath where the large net hung.

Slowly, she scanned her from left to right, the bright beam illuminating an extensive set of storage lockers along the far wall in front of her.

Outside the ship, the storm still raged in the distance. The ferocious crashes of lightning echoed as they violently struck other parts of this crater. Despite its oppressive cacophony, it was still far enough away from Beth, Perkins, and Wendy, who still stood outside the closed airlock patiently. Waiting.

"If it gets any nearer, we should probably go in," Beth had commanded, much to the annoyance of Perkins, who had earlier urged them to go in, before his failed attempts at also getting them to leave.

As Jon walked onto the bridge of the Frerichs, he noticed Davison sitting at a computer console in the dark, focused on the glowing screen in front of him. "You need more power?" Jon said as he walked up to another console on the opposite side of the room. "I found a way to get control routed up here for all the decks. "

"Please, I can't see much on just the emergency

console," Davison said with some surprise.

With a self-satisfied smirk, Jon hit a series of buttons. As he did so, the electrics across the ship burst into life. The lights on all floors quickly flickered on, and the computers on the bridge whirred and beeped as they slowly powered up.

With a smile, Jon outstretched his arms toward his commander, and proudly said, "And God said, let there be light!"

After a pause, Davison replied with a smile, "And who's God in this scenario? You?" Turning to a newly powered up computer near him, he then typed various commands into the keyboard.

Jon approached and stood behind him, looking over Davison's shoulder at the monitor.

Without turning, Davison continued, "Well, what do you think?"

"About?"

"The ship. What do you think about the ship?" Davison clarified. "I heard some of what you guys were saying on the intercom about finding some canister or something?"

Though Davison was not looking his way to see, Jon shrugged. "I'll let Susan tell you about that," he said. "As for everything else? All looks good, as much as I could see when the power was turned on. Bad news is that I couldn't find Engineering, this place is too damn big. But no obvious damage to anything I *could* see. "

"Engineering's on the second level. That's what the schematics on the emergency console said. I think… I can't do much of anything. Keep trying commands, but it's not accepting most English phrases. "

As he hit the return on the keyboard, all that came

back on the monitor was:

Fehlermeldung
Fehlermeldung
Fehlermeldung
Fehlermeldung

"What the fuck does that mean?" Jon scoffed at the German word on Davison's screen.

"I'm guessing it means *'Hell no!'*"

"Well, apart from the," Jon read the error message from the screen, "*Fell-her-a-mell-dung…* There's a bigger question. "

"What's that?"

"Where the hell's the crew?" Jon said.

"That's the million-dollar question, isn't it?" Davison stood up from the chair and walked over to an adjacent bank of computers, looking at the screens that sprang to life displaying various maps and charts.

"Could be at some dig somewhere?" Jon said.

"Maybe. But it's unlikely they'd leave the ship unattended, right?"

Jon nodded reluctantly.

Davison paused as he looked at a map on the screen, then continued, "Especially as they knew we were going to show up." He pointed to the map. On it was a map of the crater, and within it a small green dot that said *'Shenandoah'* above it.

Walking over to view the screen, Jon said in surprise, "They knew?"

"Down to the name of our ship. "

In the now-lit examination room, Susan was annoyed as she fought with the hose coupler on her helmet.

"Jesus Christ!" she said, exasperated, as she clumsily attempted to feed the hose into the coupler for a fifth time. "Who put these damn things together?"

Letting her arm fall, holding her helmet down by her side, she looked up and closed her eyes for a moment to regain her composure.

After a few seconds, to better keep balance, she put her other hand on the table in front of her – inadvertently setting it down in a pool of the slime from the cylinder.

Opening her eyes, she reacted with a grimace. She raised her hand and tried to flick the slime off from her fingers. But it stuck tight.

Placing her helmet back on the shelf, she looked around for a cloth, a tissue, *anything* to get this muck off of her.

"Typical!" she complained, disgusted at the dark matter still clinging to her palm and fingers.

Walking over to a cabinet under the examining table, she bent down and attempted to open the door by twisting its handle.

Only moving it a fraction, the handle felt sluggish. Not locked, though. Instead it felt like there was something inside fighting to keep this cabinet closed.

After gathering her strength, she yanked the handle to the left, forcing it to open.

The door flung open, as the body of an SMS Frerichs crew member fell to the floor in front of her. The skin on its wrist had been trapped within the locking mechanism of the door and had torn open from her forcing of the handle. This, though, was a minor wound compared to the devastation that had happened across almost every inch of this decaying carcass.

This poor soul's face had been mostly removed, large

claw marks gouged across its body, leaving its chest in shreds. Identifying this as a man or woman was not possible at a mere glance.

Screaming in terror, Susan scrambled backward until her back slammed into a medical locker. As she collided with it, the door to this locker pushed her forward and a second dead body tumbled outward.

As well as being dressed in the same style jumpsuit, this body shared the same signs of mauling and decay as the first. The only difference here was that its face was mostly in one piece. This man was in mid-scream. His violent death appeared to have kept his final terrified expression rigid on his face.

This corpse's wide eyes – though sunken and milky – stared out at Susan as if pleading to be saved.

Horrified, she got to her feet and bolted toward the exit, which was now closed.

In a panic, she searched for the exit button on the door's frame. Her eyes darted to the room beyond the glass, teasing the safety that lay out there. But before she could find a way out, a bizarre whine screeched from behind her.

Whirling around, she looked about the room in a panic, but all she saw were the two grotesquely mauled cadavers. Turning back to the closed door, the dread coursed through her body like acid as her breathing became more and more stilted.

Finally, she found a small black button on the wall marked *Aus*. Hoping for a miracle, she mashed her hand into the button.

In an instant, the door hissed and slid open.

With a grateful smile, Susan then squeezed herself through the gap before the door had fully opened.

She ran, forgetting that back in the examination room, on the shelf beside the table, was her helmet.

Susan had not been alone in the discovery of hidden corpses in the confines of this German vessel.

In the cargo bay, Bryce stood staring at an open storage locker in front of her. Having found various tools, rope and a multitude of computer parts in others, she had – in this last locker – discovered what now hung from its door.

The lighting, bright and on full power, had startled her when it burst to life, bathing the room. For a short time she was glad they had come on, as it enabled her to more quickly search the area. Now, though, she had wished they would have remained off. In the dark, she might have given up such a thorough exploration. She might have totally missed the corpse that now hung from the locker, and lolled to the floor.

With the new addition of a high-pitched ringing in her ears, she felt no fear about this, only annoyance with herself. She had seen countless bodies in battle, and caused many of them to be in that state herself. But here, she had not acted like her usual self. She had let her reactions get the better of her nerves. As the body lurched out from the locker, she fired off a shot toward it. That resulting shot echoed throughout the Cargo Bay and caused her to wince at the sound. To make matters worse, she had been updating Davison about her progress when it had happened, so now he was on his way from the Bridge to see what she had found.

In the Examinations Room, the bodies that had slumped to the floor from their hidden places were no longer in the same state as before. These remains were now mauled *even* further, the bodies ripped into much smaller pieces, sitting in a rotting pile of meat, bone, guts and gore.

"Susan?" Jon's voice weakly called out from the headset within Susan's helmet, still abandoned on the shelf. "You there, Susan?"

Meanwhile, Jon and Davison, having heard the noise of Bryce's gunshot over the intercom, ran down a ship's corridor, their helmets in hand.

As they approached the cargo bay, the double doors hissed open. Though Bryce had expected him, their approach had not been quiet and she would take nothing for granted on this ship. Walking out, she raised her rifle.

Quickly recognizing the commander and Davison and Jon, she lowered her weapon and nodded.

"Bryce, what the hell happened?" Davison asked.

Jon interjected, "Have you seen Susan?"

Without needing to answer any of their questions, Bryce nodded, motioning behind them down the corridor.

As they turned, they saw Susan at the far end, running frantically toward them.

"Something's killed them!" she shouted.

Unable to understand, Davison glanced at Jon. "What did she say?"

As if on cue, from the grating above them, a drop of blood fell and landed on Jon's face. Jon and Davison looked upward, and Susan's repeated scream of "Something killed them!" came into a sharp focus.

Time seemed to slow down as the grated ceiling gave way.

A dead crew member tumbled out of the ventilation shaft.

Pulling Jon out of the way just in time, Davison saved him from the falling, mangled corpse as it smashed into the floor beside them.

"Fuck!" Jon screamed, looking at Susan, who had now stopped and stared at the fallen corpse.

Terrified, she said, "Something killed them!"

Some *thing,* Davison thought.

Suddenly, Bryce raised her rifle and took a step in Susan's direction.

Horrified, Jon turned to her, but before he could say a word, Bryce let off a shot.

It reverberated down the corridor, causing Davison to grasp his ears in pain.

"No!" Jon shouted. Before he could say anything else, Susan screamed. But she had not screamed at the gunshot, or the corpse.

Standing just beyond where she cowered, at the far end of the corridor, was what Bryce had fired at; the unearthly silhouette of a large creature.

With one claw it slashed into the air, smashing the light above it, casting its presence in thick shadow.

"Run!" Davison shouted to Susan.

Unable to hold him back, Jon wrenched himself away from Davison, up the corridor to Susan, then began to drag her back toward them as she kept staring, terrified, behind them.

"What is it?" she screamed at Jon.

I missed it? Bryce chastised herself. She then took a step forward and leveled her aim again.

"Wait!" Davison commanded, but he was too late, as Bryce let off another shot.

Down the hall, the creature did not seem affected as it continued to take wide strides towards them. Every second stride was coupled with a swinging claw, which smashed the light bulbs glowing above.

Firing again, Bryce's confidence faded to confusion as she realized the other shot did indeed hit; they just had no effect on this *thing*.

"The airlock's this way!" Davison shouted as they ran as fast as they could through an open bulkhead door, away from the slowly approaching beast.

As the creature ran towards them, it dipped one arm and sliced its claws into the fallen corpses' belly. It raised a fistful of flesh to its mouth and ate it, as it came closer.

Running faster than the beast, the crew made it to the airlock.

"Jon, the override," Davison shouted loudly in a panic as he motioned for Susan and Bryce to hurry up. Jon, on his commander's order, ran into the hatch first. Standing at the control panel at the far end, he activated the door's closing mechanism.

"Helmets on!" Jon said loudly, with urgency.

As the door hissed and started to slide shut, Davison and Bryce scrambled to put their helmets on as they ran inside the fast-sealing airlock.

Susan, following from behind, halted with a look of horror on her face.

"My helmet!" she said.

In her mind she could see it, still sitting on the shelf. In the split-second she had to make it into the hatch, she paused out of self-preservation. Without a helmet, that airlock was a death trap.

Turning in a panic, she saw her oxygen feed tube, still attached at one end to her spacesuit, now dragging on the floor behind her.

The airlock door clanked as it locked closed.

Seeing through the hatch window, Davison slammed his fists against the metal.

"Susan!" he screamed, just as the airlock pressurized, sealing the helmeted crew inside.

Though he could not hear her, Davison could decipher her mouthed words of '*Help me'*.

The tears poured down her cheeks. .

Jon hit the control panel with his gloved hand. He desperately tried to cancel the pressurization and re-open the inner doors, but nothing he tried had any success.

"Why won't it fucking open?" he cried.

"Look for a manual release," Davison said.

Up on the bridge, a shadowed figure watched this scene on a monitor. From a top-down CCTV view, the figure watched Susan as she beat frantically on the closed hatch door. The black and white scene played out clearly as she broke down in fitful screams that echoed through the monitor's tinny speakers.

At the small window in the inner hatch door, Susan pleaded for help from her friends, separated by a pressurized seal.

Knowing he could not do any more at the control panel, Jon pushed past Davison and looked out at his terrified lover.

They both knew Jon could not open this door and her fate was just as sealed. The airlock's process could not be reversed with a system in a language none of them could understand.

It was only when Jon glanced over her shoulder in fear that Susan and the rest of the crew remembered the creature.

At that moment, the monster's arm smashed into the light above it, smashing it on impact and casting the corridor into darkness; the only illumination being cast from the small hatch window.

Susan had no time to turn and beg for any possible mercy from her oncoming slaughter.

As she closed her eyes, accepting the inevitable, the creature's blackened claw swung down on her like an axe. It broke its way through the top of her skull, shattering her fontanelle with incredible ease as its talon decimated her brain matter. Dr. Susan Decker's life was extinguished in an instant.

Jon, Davison, and Bryce could do nothing but witness this attack from the safety of the airlock.

As the creature took hold of the cracked edge of Susan's shattered cranium, it roared victoriously, and dragged her away.

Her body faded into the shadows, the vision of her deathly expression burned into Jon's mind; with her eyes wide and rolled upward, her mouth hung unnaturally open, forever locked in a silent scream.

"We've got to help her," Jon said as he turned to Bryce and Davison, his mind unable to comprehend what he had seen.

Barging his way back over to the control panel, again Jon tried to open the inner doors.

Bryce pulled at Jon's shoulder to stop him, but he turned and pushed her aside, slamming her into the wall of the hatch.

"She's dead, Jon!" Davison said, pleading "There's nothing we can do!"

Jon shrugged off the hand that Davison put on his shoulder, and kept pressing different combinations of buttons into the panel.

On the bridge, the shrouded figure still watched the monitor. The display had changed to a view from inside the hatch. The figure watched Jon scream at his crewmates, "We can still save her!"

With her rifle over her shoulder, Bryce grabbed a small metal pistol from her belt, then aimed it at Jon. At the same time, Davison wrapped his arms around Jon from the back, trying to restrain him.

As she fired, a small object flew out from the gun and struck Jon's helmet, sticking to its glass visor.

"Let him go now," she shouted to Davison, who only had a second before the device emitted a strong electrical pulse. It sparked wildly for a heartbeat, then Jon slumped to the floor, unconscious.

"He'll be alright," Bryce said. "Just a light tranquilizer. Should last only a few seconds at most." She put the pistol back on her belt and grabbed her rifle off her shoulder.

Jon started muttering; he was starting to wake up.

"Help me get him up," Davison said to Bryce, as they moved Jon into an upright seated position.

At that moment, the outer doors made a loud screech as they slid upward, letting the elements of Titan blow in.

Standing just outside the open door, Perkins, Beth and Wendy looked in.

Beth was first to notice something amiss. "What the hell happened?" she said, as she saw the blood covering the inner door's glass.

Perkins looked at Jon, now waking up.

"What happened to Jon?" Wendy said. "And where's

Susan?"

Chapter Five
The Titan Find

Davison's mind was a whirl. He knew that heading back to the Shenandoah was merely delaying a death sentence for them all. Their ship was simply not viable to take them back to Earth, and had a finite oxygen supply.

Though they should be able to exist there for a while, the chance of a rescue ship coming to get them was slim to none. They *were* the rescue ship, besides NTI would never spend an additional fortune launching a second rescue mission.

Their only hope was retrieving as many of their weapons as they could, then attempting to commandeer the Richter Dynamics ship from the grips of... of that *thing*...

He couldn't bring himself to think that this *really* was an alien. That very idea was insane. *Wasn't it?* Wendy posited that there *could* be aliens. That they *could* have killed the geologists of the Titan find. But it was all so far-fetched. All the extraterrestrial evidence humanity had discovered dated to way back before the dinosaurs had roamed the Earth. Thus, having a creature from another world here, attacking them… Well, it was as ludicrous to Davison as discovering a T-Rex alive and well on the shores of Miami.

Maybe it wasn't even an alien, Davison thought. *Maybe it was some kind of genetic weapon?* Something built on Titan, out of the watch of the governmental sanctions on weaponized lifeforms. *That* was more likely.

"Commander," Perkins said to Davison, who again walked at the head of the group. "This could have all been avoided, you know? I *did* say we should all bring weapons. Didn't I—"

"Shut the fuck up, Perkins," Davison retorted, not even turning to address him. "This isn't the goddamn time for your bullshit. "

Perkins looked smug. He had made the commander break. This man, who relied on his calm nature to lead, had snapped at him.

On the bridge of the SMS Frerichs, a hand reached out and typed a command into the computer's keyboard;

Abschalten_1_2_3_4-5AUF

As the return key was pressed, the entire spaceship – bar the bridge – was cast into the same darkness it had been consumed by before. Before the American crew had stirred the beast.

Somewhere on the lower levels, hidden within the darkest shadows, a human head had been removed from its mutilated body. This head – once that of Dr. Susan Decker – now rested in the beast's monstrous claw. Lifting the head up to its mouth, its mandible opened wide enough to fit the cranium in - resembling a snake eating a large bird. With Susan's decapitated head halfway inside its maw, its jaw clamped down tight with a terrifying force. Its teeth tore through the skull with immense ease, biting into her brain pan in one motion.

The abhorrent sounds of this beast's chewing echoed down the ship's dark, desolate corridors.

* * * * *

The American crew stood on the dungeon-like terrain in the middle of a strange underground cavern. All the caverns they traversed were alien and surreal, but this one was significantly less recognizable than the others, with no long, snaking rocks or Swiss-cheese looking slabs anywhere to be seen. Instead, immense blood-red stalactites and stalagmites towered around them, creating the illusion that they were standing in the middle of a giant's fanged mouth.

High above them, the cavern ceiling had long, thick cracks in it, which exposed the lightning's brightness in wide flashing shafts, down onto where they stood.

"Just under half," Beth said to Jon as she read the oxygen level on the canister attached to the back of his spacesuit. "You're doing fine. "

With a weak smile, Jon carried on walking. He still looked as though he couldn't accept what had happened, what he had seen with his own two eyes.

Up ahead, Davison slowed down. "Hold up," he said with a raised fist, signalling them to follow suit.

Obeying the command, the crew slowed to a stop – except Perkins, who strode forward to Davison.

"Why the hell are you stopping, Commander?" he said pointedly, as if wanting to create a scene.

Davison glanced around the unfamiliar terrain and replied, "None of this looks familiar. Does it to you?"

"That's nonsense," Perkins said as he surveyed their location. "I'm sure we—" His face fell and his words trailed off. Realization dawned on him that Davison was indeed correct.

"You're right," Wendy said. "We should be at those

black rocks by now."

With frustration bubbling up inside, Perkins exploded as he shouted, "We're fuckin' lost? *This is not acceptable*!"

Wendy shook her head at the outburst.

Perkins continued his tirade. "You have put us in jeopardy *one too many times*. That's it! I'm taking command."

Davison calmly replied, not allowing himself to lose his temper again at this man - this corporate representative. "Mr. Perkins. You're not taking control of anything. So," Turning to his crew, he finished this thought, by reiterating what he had said earlier – but this time without anger or even a raised tone – "...shut the fuck up."

Not letting it go, Perkins stormed in front of the commander, squaring up to him. "*You* smashed the ship," he railed, getting louder with every word. "You deemed it *wise* to override *my* orders, and *not* go to an enemy vessel armed. Then you get one of your crew *killed*, and now... *Now*—"

"You best close your goddamn mouth," Bryce said in a curt and gruff tone. Her rifle was aimed at Perkins, its barrel pressed against the side of his helmet's visor. "You are talking to the commander of this mission. *He* is in charge."

Perkins stared at the end of the rifle with a mix of repressed anger and fear. As he was about to reply, Bryce cut in again. "Shut up, before I blow your face off," she continued with a disgusted tone. "You're a fucking worm, do you understand? Not one more word."

Davison looked at her, surprised and amused.

Perkins nodded meekly, feeling a deep betrayal.

With a smirk, Bryce lowered her weapon.

"Jon?" Davison called out, taking the focus off this event, to a more pressing matter. But Jon looked vacant of any traces of emotion. He stared blanky forward.

"Jon," Davison said louder. "You bring the homing device with you?"

Jon just stared, trying to find the words amongst the anguish.

"Jon?" Davison reiterated even louder.

After a beat, Jon smiled. An apologetic and heartbroken smile. "It's… I left it... back... Su—"

Before he could bring himself to say her name, Jon's words caught in his throat.

"That's okay." Davison said. "We probably don't need it. We just gotta carefully backtrack, that's all. "

From the corner of her eyes, Wendy saw something flash that piqued her interest.

Davison watched her as she walked over to the side of the rock face, that ended in a sheer drop, down to a lower cavern.

"Can't be that hard to find where we took a wrong turn," Beth said.

"Commander?" Wendy whispered, though loud enough to be picked up by her microphone.

"What are you seeing over there?" Davison asked.

Wendy glanced over her shoulder. "There's something..." she turned back to the lower cavern. "I think you better take a look at it. "

Walking over to her side, Davison glanced over the edge. He silently took in the sight ahead of him, then said, "I guess we're going down there then. "

* * * * *

The Titan find.

On this lower level, the remnants of the Shenandoah's crew stood open-mouthed ahead of the metal and stone structure towering up in front of them.

Surrounded by a dozen powerless floodlights, diggers, drills and other machines, the several terraced levels of what had been excavated stuck out from the rocks. The lightning from the cracks in the earth above lit up the area in small narrow bursts.

The flashlights on the crew's suits did nothing to reveal much of what was clearly of alien origin. This structure's high metal pillars seemed to lightly pulse from within with a dull blue glow.

Beyond a man-made entranceway carved into the rock at the bottom of the structure, a corridor was visible, with a blue glow emanating from within.

Tentatively, Davison walked toward this entrance, followed by the others. As he got closer, the glow seemed to slowly change to a lighter hue.

Perkins stared up at the structure as he followed, unable to contain his glee. "This is it!" he said in awe. "We found it!"

"State the obvious much?" Beth said with sarcasm as she walked past him, following behind Davison, who had now walked through the entraceway.

Before joining the rest of the crew inside, Wendy – ever-curious – walked over to one of the large pillars to examine it more closely. Though made of solid metal, it had veins running through it that pulsed with an unnatural luminescence. As she walked closer, the light shifted in reaction. Making a perfect silhouette of Wendy the closer she got to it, the pillar's glow grew darker as if reflecting her shadow.

Smiling at this, Wendy turned to show her crew, but they were all gone. Into the structure. Fearing being alone anymore, she hurriedly followed them in.

"Nearly half a million years old," Perkins said to himself in awe as he looked around the corridor. The structure's original metal walls had been excavated from under the stone, and now they displayed not only strange mechanisms built in them – tubes, wires and other electronics that spread over its fascia – but also uncovered doorways leading to other smaller rooms.

"This will be worth a *fortune*," Perkins continued, looking like a child in a toy store.

"Only if we make it back," Bryce quipped, making sure Perkins realized she was still watching him.

Looking at one wall, Davison noticed that there were shaped indentations in the metal, as if things had been removed. His mind was cast back to the room in the German ship with the strange objects lined up on the tables. *So they've stripped this place already*, he thought.

"It reminds me of my old research laboratory," Wendy said from behind as she ran her hand over the coldness of the wall. "Some of this stuff might still work... and these..." She moved over to a large section of uncovered walls, where a series of large broken cylinders rested in their own cubbyhole-like slots, each with a dull blue glow emanating from within.

"What are those glass things?" Bryce asked, motioning to the cylinders with her rifle, still tightly gripped in her hands.

"No idea." Wendy shrugged. "Specimen jars? or environmental containers? Like to grow food in. No way of knowing without proper analysis. "

Beth shrugged. "Too bad they're broken. "

"Maybe that's a *good* thing." Bryce chuckled.

Jon looked silently to the cylinders, mute with grief.

Davison peered into a few of the cylinders still in their cubby-holes. He could see some plant growths in one, others had dried residues of multiple colors around their cracked edges. "Looks like there could have been different things in each of them. "

Bryce, on the lookout, walked to the end of the corridor, still in security mode.

"Doc," Davison asked as he turned to Wendy. "Don't suppose these things could have held something still alive, could they?"

Wendy looked confused for a moment. "You mean the thing on the ship?" she said, then looked to the cubby-holes. "Only if they were hermetically sealed, and held in a state of suspended animation."

Davison exhaled. This information was both fascinating and terrifying.

"But none of this seems to have power. "

"What do you mean?" Perkins asked, pointing to the blue glow coming from the holes. "There is clearly still power. "

"I think that is not power, but some kind of bioluminescence. Nothing could be powered for thousands of years without a fuel. So this glow… has to be natural… Then again…"

Davison turned to Wendy, waiting on her next words. "Then again?" he prompted.

"Then again, I'm not an alien scientist. I, frankly, don't know. At all. In the slightest. I'm just spit-balling here. It's all just educated guesses."

Beth walked over to a cracked cylinder which lay on the dirt floor near to the wall of cubby-holes.

"Susan found a glass thing like that on the ship," Jon said weakly.

Wendy turned to him and said, "Was it empty?"

Jon shrugged.

"I have no idea why they would take one with them, unless there was something in it. "

Wendy walked over to Beth as she examined the casing of the removed cylinder. She rubbed the dirt from the top of its glass, then aimed her flashlight inside, illuminating the black residue that sat within. Along its side, she noticed a dried, brownish-red smear.

"That's not blood, is it?" she said to Wendy, who did not answer as she tried to focus on the residue in the cylinder.

Walking blindly to the far side of the object, Beth gasped and threw herself backward against an adjacent wall.

Wendy peered over the cylinder Beth was still staring at.

Lying in the dirt was the remains of another dead astronaut. One with an NTI space suit on. Its helmet was shattered. The remaining glass shards of the visor were encrusted with blood. This corpse's face was a decayed vision of horror.

Wendy's hand shot up to her mask, as if to cover her mouth.

Davison rushed around and caught sight of the dead body. He said with urgency, "It's not confined to their ship, we have to leave. NOW. "

"At least we know that our men did not survive," Perkins said, nonchalantly. "...And the Germans were indeed here to steal our find. "

Beth turned to the commander, and in uncharacteristic panic said, "What the hell happened here?. "

"C'mon," Davison said. "Less time spent here, the better." He looked at Bryce. "You take the lead back to the ship. "

With a nod, Bryce held her rifle up in a defensive stance, then walked past the others. Davison ushered them all to follow.

Chapter Six
The Fallen Daughter

Before Davison had been given command of the Shenadoah, he had hoped for a *Journeypath* class starship; one of the brand-new hybrid exploration/battle crafts that would have made his fellow commanders green with envy. Those ten-level crafts were fitted with the latest holo-tech interfaces, advanced AI simulators and came standard with a fleet of six, two person mini-crafts.

Instead, he had been issued a *Shaman* class ship; one that was significantly older than he wanted. But any paid command was good enough to take. He didn't *need* the work after all, but the pay NTI offered was – as always – far above the market rate, especially when needed to fly beyond Mars, for which they routinely offered double pay.

Mission Controller Gos Thompson had handed him the contract to sign. On it, Davison noticed the name of the craft he was given. *The Shenandoah*. Having never heard the word before, he asked about its meaning.

The controller simply smiled and told him that when he was head of NTI's marketing division, he had re-named all NTI vessels.

"So many of the ships had such awful names. Names like a child thought them up. So, I decided I needed to rebrand the whole fleet. "

"And why the Shenandoah?" Davison asked.

"Off the Potomac, the Shenandoah was once a river that ran past my family home in Blue Ridge, Virginia." His tone turned mournful. "Until the waters finally dried up. That was around the time my mother was carrying me. "

Davison nodded, but Gos was not finished.

"The name itself comes from my Father's ancestors; the Algonquin Indians. He loved to tell me of their old language, and regarding Shenandoah, it roughly translates as," his face broke into a smile as he said, "the beautiful daughter of the stars. "

Davison couldn't help but return a smile as he replied, "Bad name for a river, but for a spaceship? Goddamn perfect if you ask me. "

"I always thought so too. But you're the first to ask about what the word means, and I thank you for that. "

The beautiful daughter of the stars? Hearing that made Davison glad he *wasn't* given a *Journeypath* class ship.

He signed the contract gladly.

* * * * *

The Shenandoah now lay lifeless in the shadows of the expansive cavern. Occasional lightning flashed down through the hole in the ceiling far overhead. The only real illumination down there.

Since the time the crew had left to venture to the German craft, the hole in the surface had begun to expand at a significantly faster rate. Initially split open by the weight of the ship's landing, the ceiling had now lost nearly all its strength. Rocks around its rim began to break away, then tumble downward.

After they had found a path back from the Titan find, the crew now stood in front of their ship. Looking at it in shock at what had changed since they had seen it last. The debris from the surface had fallen down onto the ship so, slowly but surely, the Shenandoah had begun to be buried. It was as if this moon had known that the spaceship was broken beyond repair, and had taken it upon itself to perform the last rites, and become its de facto gravedigger.

This defeated vessel, mostly covered in red rock, slowly leaked various gasses from exposed lines that had ruptured from Titan filling in its grave.

* * * * *

Within the middle Cargo Bay, Beth – back in her jumpsuit – sat against some large metal boxes. With her knees pulled up to her chest, she rested her head on her folded arms. Her cheeks were stained with dry tears.

She glanced at the line of open lockers next to the internal door leading to the ship. In each one, the space suits the crew had worn on their recent excursion now hung. She stared at the one empty locker; Susan's.

The lights were on, but were very dim. Like the SMS Frerichs, this craft had now been placed under emergency conditions, with all machinery either turned off or in low-power mode. All in order to conserve as much power as possible.

Beth listened to the storm from up on the Moon's surface. Its cacophony echoed throughout the cavern like a distant artillery.

When they had arrived back, they had been relieved to find out that despite the heavy battery from the falling rocks, the structural integrity for most of the Shenandoah was still good. With only four compromised areas that needed sealing off, Beth knew they should be counting themselves lucky, though she couldn't help but think an inescapable death was worse than a sudden death.

Breaking into her thoughts, the whirring sound of the internal doors to the cargo bay opening stole her from her misery. The low light from the corridor drifted in and illuminated her face.

"You ok?" Davison asked Beth, crouching down in front of her.

She nodded unconvincingly.

"It'll work out... somehow," he said, just as unconvincingly. He continued, "Nobody's on the bridge."

"Oh?" Beth replied. "You need me up there?"

"No," Davison shook his head. "I didn't mean that. I just couldn't find anybody, that's all."

"I think Wendy's with Jon on the observation deck."

"What about Bryce and Perkins?" he said. "Any ideas?"

She took a breath. She hated the fact she felt weak and hated that Davison saw her in this condition.

"Bryce said she was going to her quarters... and Perkins," she shrugged instead of finishing off her sentence.

Davison noticed she had been crying. "And where are you then?" he asked kindly.

Managing a small smile, Beth replied, "I'm here, El Commandante, don't you worry. Just taking in everything, that's all."

"Understood." With a nod, Davison stood back up. "I'm gonna go talk to Jon. See what our options are."

"I'm guessing what we saw *was* oxygen leaking out?" Beth said, though she knew the answer.

"Yeah. I managed to stop the leak, but—" He paused. "Well, it's not good. Not good at all."

Beth broke eye contact and looked down at her arms, now comfortingly folded over her chest. "Between Susan and this place, it's like a bad fucking dream. "

He didn't reply, but Davison's expression confirmed that he felt the same.

Weakly, Beth asked, "We're gonna die, aren't we?"

Snapping out of any maudlin attitude, Davison smiled confidently. "No. I can't let that happen." Before Beth could call him a liar, he continued, "Look, I need you to do something for me. But we haven't got much time. Call it our Hail Mary. "

She looked up at him.

"Can you put together a KFM transmitter out of stuff we have on the ship? If we can somehow cut through this interference and get a message to Concorde, or to home..." He paused, as if trying to convince himself that it was a realistic idea. "Maybe, just *maybe*, they could re-route a ship to come get us. "

"You're not serious, right?"

He persisted. "If we don't try absolutely *everything*, then we could miss an opportunity. A one percent chance of success is way better than a hundred percent chance of failure, right?"

"I'd have to rip some stuff out from the main computer. What about the air supply? Even if we could get a message through-"

"Don't you worry about that. I've got an idea that might buy us some time, or at least keep us occupied. "

* * * * *

In the half-light of Bryce's room, she had stacked several large weapon cases on top of each other. All of them were made of a gray rugged plastic, emblazoned on their sides with a white NTI logo. The lack of illumination caused the room to be heavily coated in shadows, giving a hazy twilight look.

On the desk next to her bunk, half a dozen large pistols were lined up neatly in a row, with a couple of dozen boxes of ammunition piled at the end.

She dragged a large open-topped wooden crate from under her desk, and glanced over the various pieces of surveillance equipment that were stacked within. When everything seemed in order, she nodded to herself, then moved the box next to the weapons crates.

Walking to her locker, next to the closed door, she unzipped the front of her jumpsuit. As she pulled it from her shoulders, she could not help but think of the creature, and how it had been unfazed by her shots. As she stepped one leg out of the jumpsuit, her eyes widened. She heard a slight noise behind her. Almost nothing.

Almost.

Lifting out her other leg, she picked up the worn jumpsuit then threw it onto the bunk.

Wearing only her underwear and a thin leather bracelet around her wrist, she stood.

Paused.

Waiting.

Listening for another noise.

Slowly, she unbuttoned the bracelet on her wrist, then held one end of it, leaving the other to dangle downward.

Within an instant, a grease-stained hand shot out from the shadows behind her, then clasped her tightly around the neck.

"Shhhhhh" came a gruff, heavily accented male voice

from the shadows. As he spoke, he pulled her closer.

A craggy-faced man in a Richter Dynamics space suit – without a helmet -

moved his face close to her ear then whispered, "I am not here to hurt you. "

Bryce struggled, but as she tried to break free, his grip tightened.

"I said, I would not hurt you," he repeated through gritted teeth, as he strained to keep her still.

Glancing around, he noticed all the pistols on the desk. "Looks like I may have chosen the wrong person to introduce myself to, eh?" he said with a lighter tone in his voice.

As she pushed her weight back, this man steadied himself from toppling over and screamed in her ear.

"Stop!" he commanded, as he increased the grip on her throat.

Instantly she ceased pushing back, knowing to not push further.

He then slightly relaxed his hand and smiled. "See? Not difficult," he said softly.

She grimaced as she waited for her turn to come.

"I will take my hand off you now." His voice carried with it a sudden tinge of lasciviousness.

In her hand, Bryce firmly gripped her bracelet.

"I see you like guns," he said as he moved his hand from her neck and stroked her cheek from behind. "What else do you like, mein Fräulein?"

Through a gritted smile she replied, "You really want to know?"

His smile widened like a Cheshire Cat's, as his other hand traced up the side of her body and made its way over her ribs, towards her breasts. "Of course I want to know.

Tell me."

"I like..." she said, now ready to transform from a fly into a spider. "...I like violence."

With a flick of her wrist, she snapped the bracelet outward. What was seemingly a leather strap now became a straight, solid object; a hidden weapon within the accessory.

She pressed the metal clasp on the bracelet, which depressed with a click, causing a thin metal blade to spring out of the now-solid handle.

Before the German intruder could react, Bryce lifted her foot back with force, connecting with his groin, sending him slumped to the floor.

Spinning around, she grasped this intruder's unruly blond hair, yanked his head back and thrust her blade up to his throat, ready to slice at any notice.

Through the shooting pain in his groin, this man looked strangely happy.

"You are *my* kind of woman," he said.

Moments later, he lost consciousness as Bryce's fist collided with his temple.

* * * * *

The craggy-faced German astronaut sat on an examination table in the medical bay. Still dressed in his filthy, stained space suit, he looked dazed. Drops of blood from a wound above his left temple streaked down his face.

He glanced at the Americans standing around him, listened patiently as the man who had introduced himself as Commander Davison asked the female doctor where one of the crew were.

"I gave him a sedative," she replied. "He's resting."

Turning to the German, she held an antiseptic wipe up to his head wound. As she looked into his strangely empty eyes, she felt unsettled.

She began to dab the blood from his temple. "It'll probably leave a scar, but if you just put a little makeup over it, you can—" Glancing at him, she noticed he was not even looking at her anymore; or listening. He was, instead, staring at Bryce with a wide smile. But she was showing him no emotion in return.

Turning to Davison, the man laughed as he motioned to Bryce. "She is very good, this one. Like a Valkyrie."

"If she was really trying, you'd be dead," Davison said with no trace of humor in his voice. "You understand that, right?"

Shooing Wendy away with one hand, the man then moved off the examination table, straightened up, and winced with pain. He held his side as he looked again at Bryce. "You got some cheap shots in, huh? Whilst I was unconscious?"

Davison had had enough of the pleasantries and walked up to this stranger. A clear foot taller than the diminutive German, Davison towered over him, and glared.

"Okay, enough of this. Who are you?" he demanded.

Answering as he glanced at the others in the room, the German showed no trace of being intimidated. "My name is Hans Rudi Hofner. Demolitions. Richter Dynamics." He turned his icy gaze up to Davison. "At your service, Commander Davison."

"Hofner?" Davison asked.

Hofner bared his teeth with a wide grin. "I feel like

we are family now. No need to be so formal. Rudi, please. "

None of the American crew looked amused by this exchange. Beth seemed slightly worried. Bryce's expression was – as ever – unreadable. Wendy looked annoyed and Perkins, unsurprisingly, appeared incensed.

"How did you get in here?" Davison did not have time to play this strange man's games.

"Well, in case you didn't notice, the rear of your spacecraft is..." Hofner searched for the right word. "ist weg... . uhh missing! Yes. It is missing, gone. I came in through there. "

"Who is with you?" Davison asked without letting the man pause for air.

"Excuse me? Who? No one. I am alone. "

"And where's your helmet?"

"It is by the airlock. Look, you *need* to trust me. I mean you no harm. "

Bryce's expression broke ever so slightly, as a razor-thin smirk appeared on her stoic expression.

After a pause, Hofner continued. "Now, who was the clever person that thought to land on this broken ground?"

Perkins spoke up, before anyone had the chance to put that blame rightly on his shoulders. "I think you need to understand, Herr Hofner, that your position here is tenuous at best. Frankly, I'd just as soon throw you back outside and save the air. Now tell us what we want to know. "

"You misunderstand me," Hofner said apologetically.

"What exactly do we misunderstand?" Davison asked, trying to stop emotions running too high.

Hofner explained, "I'm only here to help, you see?

We all require the same thing... To get off this rock with breath still in our lungs... yes?"

"How could you possibly help us?" Perkins asked, his lip curled.

"Simple. I know something you don't know. "

"And what's that?" Davison said, dreading the answer.

"I watched you on the Frerichs. I saw you. I saw that *you* saw the… monster, you called it?"

"You saw us and didn't help?" Beth asked.

Hofner ignored her question, yet spoke his next words directly at her. "I know what you were up against." He turned back to Davison. "And I have a plan to destroy it."

Perkins snorted as he waved his hand toward Hofner. "I wouldn't trust you any farther than I could throw you. "

Beth chimed in, much to her own annoyance. "For once I agree with you. "

Without breaking his eye contact with Davison, Hofner said softly, "It is a good thing they are not in charge, isn't it, Commander?"

Without pausing, Davison said, "And exactly what is it you think we're up against?"

He grinned smugly; Hofner then raised his hand, placed it on his forehead and ran it slowly down his face.

As his palm moved over his happy features, his expression changed. Shifted as if he was performing for a child. This new expression, one of great gravitas.

Every crew member of the Shenandoah thought the same thing: this man was not mentally stable.

"Maybe I *shouldn't* tell you," Hofner said in a deathly serious tone. "You are all cruel to me…" In a surreal movement, he turned his head around in a circle, his expression switching back to happiness, "Except I have no choice but to trust you. I have no option."

He then continued, "That place back there, the place I followed you from. The place with the glass pods... Do you *realise* what that place is?" He paused for effect. "Kopieranstalt tresor." He knew that none of these people understood his words, so he rephrased. "We have found someone's private collection. A collection of life from all over this - and other - galaxies... It is like a small child's butterfly collection."

Davison pictured all the cylinders in their cubby-holes. Though this man was indeed strange and unstable, Davison believed his words.

Hofner continued, "And some of these butterflies? They are not so friendly... You see? When we landed, there were thirty-two men and women. Now… Now there is only me. Hans Rudi Hofner."

Unlike the commander, Perkins did not believe this man. "How do we know you didn't kill them all?"

"And Susan," Beth added.

Hofner turned to them with a look of disgust on his face. "Don't be infantile," he spat.

Bryce said, "And the man at the excavation?"

Shaking his head, Hofner sat back down on the edge of the examination table. "When we first arrived, we made the mistake of bringing aboard the only unbroken pod we could see, and as much of the find as we could remove."

"And?" Perkins asked flippantly.

"Do you think I'd come here, if I *had* killed them? I could fly away on my own. But some of you saw the creature we are up against."

Clearly, nothing this man could say would convince

Perkins to do anything except distrust him.

Hofner continued anyway, "*My friends* were on that ship. But one by one they died... killed by something that had waited over *four thousand* centuries for them. And now... it waits for *us*. But it does not just pounce like a lion. It infects the dormant mind with its poison, asleep or or dead. It takes hold of a man, and leads him into damnation! It thought it had me at one point. But I? I was too smart for it. I broke free. "

Perkins looked at Davison. He had had enough of this madness. "Why don't we just go back to my original plan? Secure the ship section by section... Bryce here can blast it to hell and—"

Davison interrupted. "Her weapons had no effect last time. What makes you think it would be different now?"

"This creature is not dumb," Hofner protested. "You can't fight it on your terms. We have to draw it out of the ship; we must do this now, not later. It is why I came here. I have explosives on my ship that can blow it to the rings of Saturn. But I cannot lead it into a trap by myself. "

"Why did you attack Bryce then?" Beth asked, almost looking to start a fight.

"I could not help myself. You see, I…. I fell asleep. And that *thing* forced me to..." he paused as his smile returned and he turned to Bryce, changing the subject. "...It was exciting, though. Don't you think so? A bit of adrenaline to liven things up?"

Turning with a jolt back toward Davison, Hofner asked, "Will you help me, Commander, yes?"

"I'll think it over," Davison replied.

"I love you," a disembodied voice whispered

through the fog.

Jon knew that voice was Susan's.

"Where are you?" he heard himself reply, but could not feel himself actually *speaking* the words. All he could feel was the chill of the swirling mist around him.

Looking down, he noticed he was wearing his spacesuit. How did he get here? Where was Susan? His hands moved up to his face, and he felt the glass on the front of his helmet.

"Jon?" the unseen voice said. "Don't you love me?"

"Of course I do, where are you?" he said.

His head darted from left to right, trying to see where she was.

"I'm here, Jon." The voice remained soft. "You left me, but I didn't die. "

Jon's eyes burst open as he awoke with a start from his dream.

Blinking hard, his eyes quickly focused as he remembered that he had fallen asleep below the window in the observation bay. Wendy had given him something to help. And it did help. Fast.

Wendy wanted him to sleep in his bunk, but it had to be here; the place where he and Susan last made love.

With his dream fading, he felt a gnawing, unwelcome pang of grief slip into his mind. Closing his eyes for a moment, he tried to push those emotions deep down where he could not feel them.

From outside the window, flashes of lightning pulsed from high above on the moon's surface, their flickering glow cascading down through the broken hole, their blue and white light breaking into the dim observation bay.

He sat staring at the frame of the window, watching as a reflected pulse from the storm illuminated the frame's white painted metal.

Taking a deep breath he thought, *Pull yourself out of it, she wouldn't want you to be like this.*

Turning his head, he looked out of the window, hoping that the falling debris had slowed, allowing the Shenandoah to avoid being totally buried. Instead his gaze met with the ghostly and impossible form of Susan.

Standing on rocks, thirty feet from the window, Susan stared back. Without clothing, her skin was a pale beacon against the cavern's dark hue.

Her face carried the same expression as when Jon had seen her last; eyes rolled back, mouth agape in a silent scream. It expressed the immense pain and perpetual torment she'd felt in her last moments. The top of her head was split wide open; the damage caused from the monster's claw. From this deathly wound, blood stained her porcelain skin in streaks down her body.

Around her, the swirling mist that lined the cavern slowly began to creep up, until it enveloped her completely.

The mist then began to rise off the floor and cover the window he stood at - rising until nothing could be seen except its whiteness.

As he watched helplessly, he then noticed that the mist had somehow breached the airtight seal of the window, and was now beginning to seep in.

Unable to move, he could only stare as this poison fog forced its way in and over him. As it forced its way into his lungs, the methane and hydrogen cyanide that made up the mist somehow did not erode his insides. After the initial shock, he found he could breathe it like oxygen.

"I'm sorry," he managed to say as tears filled his eyes. He couldn't figure out if what he was enduring was a dream or reality.

Through these thick clouds he again heard Susan's voice, "Come find me, Jon. I'm waiting." Her words sounded as if she had spoken them next to his ear. She felt so close.

"Come to me," she said. "Just press it, Jon. Press it. "

Standing in the pressurized airlock hatch, Jon was dressed in his full spacesuit. He raised his hand and pressed the button to release the outer doors.

His eyes were closed.

He was lost in a dream.

Deep in his mind, he was still in the observation bay, hearing Susan's words of comfort. "Don't you see, Jon? I cannot be taken away from you. We are meant to be. Always and forever. "

"The creature was using us for *food*... but it was selective," Hofner said, still in the medical bay being questioned by the crew. "It used some of us to kill our own. Confusing us. Playing tricks with our eyes and minds. "

"Tricks?" Davison said. "How do you mean, tricks?"

Hofner replied, "How else? It controlled them all. Like puppets. Mentally, physically, however it could. Wherever you were weakest. "

Perkins shook his head. He did not know why they were even entertaining the notions this man spouted. He would be classed as – according to the consensus of NTI management –an enemy combatant, and should be treated as such.

Davison said, "I don't understand this control thing.

How can it do that?"

"Commander," Hofner said with an air of urgency in his voice. "Please don't try to understand this beast. We *have* to kill it... you know... there is no other way. We cannot capture and study it, find out the how and the why. "

"Oh come on," Perkins said. "Who do you think you are to demand that?"

Hofner turned to Wendy who stood by his side. "Thank you very much for your treatment and your kindness, Frau Doctor. I apologize if I have been… difficult. "

He stood up from the examination table, then asked, "Can you tell me where your facilities are? I need to relieve myself. "

"I'll escort him," Bryce said, picking up the rifle.

Davison nodded.

Hofner smiled as Bryce motioned with her free hand for him to exit first. Her other hand gripped her rifle firmly.

"Keep your comms open," Davison said.

"You don't trust me, Commander?" Hofner asked as he chuckled then walked out of the room.

"I'll keep him in line," Bryce said as she followed the German out.

After a few moments of looking toward the doorway, ensuring their guest was gone, Perkins turned back to Davison. "That man is *not* to be trusted."

"He's certifiable, sure," Davison replied. "But I don't agree. I get the impression he's telling the truth. At least what he *believes* the truth to be. "

"You cannot be serious, he's a lunatic who probably slaughtered his own crew!" Perkins spoke in a hushed voice, cautious that the German might overhear him. Despite his bravado and firm opinions, Perkins was clearly afraid of the man.

Davison turned to Beth. "How 'bout you? What d'you think?"

"I dunno, but I dread to think what he meant by *relieving himself*," Beth muttered.

"Okay," Davison then turned to Wendy. "What do you think, Doc?"

She knew full well what the real question here was. It was not merely if she believed this visitor or not, but – more importantly – was she siding with Perkins.

"The man is clearly still in shock," Wendy said plainly. "He's badly malnourished. Is hyper-deprived of sleep. He—"

Beth interrupted and said to Davison, "Do *you* believe that that thing made people turn on each other?"

Davison shrugged. "Who knows what to believe? But at the end of the day, he has obviously experienced more of this place than we have. "

"Commander," Perkins said. "You cannot—"

"Let me finish," Davison said, stopping Perkins' tirade in its tracks. "Whether it is true or not, is frankly beside the point. Us calling him a liar does nothing to help the situation. He *said* he has explosives. He *said* he has a plan. How about we just give him the benefit of the doubt, until we learn otherwise? As long as we keep our wits about ourselves, we should not be at a disadvantage. "

"One percent chance of success, better than a hundred percent chance of failure?" Beth recalled, finally understanding his approach.

Davison smiled and nodded. "Exactly. "

His shoulders slumped, Perkins gave up the

argument.

"I'm going to check in on Jon," Wendy said as she pointed from Davison to Perkins "Now you two... play nice, okay?"

The poison mist that had built up outside of the ship crept in through the outer airlock door, filling the empty hatch with its thick haze. The lights upon the control panel flicked brightly from green to red, as they signaled the door's imminent closing.

Across the cavern, Jon walked in a dream-like state.

His feet, though unsteady over the uneven ground, kept him moving.

His eyes remained closed, his mouth half-open.

"You are doing so well," Susan's dulcet tones whispered dreamily into his ear.

Suddenly, he was lying naked on a pillow inside the observation bay. Not alone, as Susan was beside him - unharmed and very much alive.

She moved over his naked body, kissing his bare chest on the way downward.

Though his unconscious body had walked out of the confines of the cavern - leaving his mind in this dream - Jon somehow knew that Susan was indeed dead. He knew in his heart that she was not with him in the observation room. That despite what his mind was showing him, she was only a memory.

He did not know, however, that he was currently sleepwalking towards the SMS Frerichs.

In his mindscape, within the safety of the ship, Jon glanced down at Susan as she stared back up at him, her hand firmly grasping his erection. Her eyes were wide, bright and animal-like. Hungry.

This may have only been a dream, and she may indeed not really be here, but at this moment, Jon did not care.

Chapter Seven
Under the Influence

The Richter Dynamics ship loomed up high, bathed in thick shadows like a Gothic castle. Devoid of any power, it was a monolith within this desolate landscape. As with Jonathan Harker's arrival at Castle Dracula, Jon was ambivalent to the danger swelling within his destination.

Lost in the confines of a dream, Jon stood at the foot of the ship and looked up, though with eyes still closed, for his view was not for *his* eyes to see. Something else saw through them. Guide him.

"Come to me." Susan's disembodied voice spoke to his unconsciousness, as his conscious mind was still deep in its carnal dream. With her words bleeding in from his dreams, his body had no way to stop him saying aloud, "I love you, Susan."

With the airlock now closed behind him and the inner door open, Jon walked into the darkness of the German ship. As that door closed behind him, a vault-like thud echoed down the corridor. Without any conscious thought, he removed his helmet, then dropped it without care to the metal floor. As it landed, it rolled onto its side, smearing the glass with a red liquid that had been on the floor. These remnants; the lifeblood that had fallen from his love only a few hours earlier.

With one foot heavily placed in front of another, Jon

walked down the corridor in his slumber.

Through the maze of twists and turns, through dark passageways and up flights of metal steps, Jon eventually arrived at the door to the ship's bridge.

In his dream, in the observation bay, reaching a mutual crescendo of ecstasy, Jon and Susan moaned together loudly; simultaneously climaxing as they held each other tightly.

It was here that Jon was stolen from his dream and awoke on the German ship.

With his eyes wide open, Jon found himself standing on the bridge of the SMS Frerichs. The lights in this room were off, but some of the computers were on and running, their blinking lights casting a faint glow into the surrounding darkness. They cast dull flickers outward, lending the room a surreal and foreboding look.

His breathing shallow and growing rapid, Jon stared at the silhouette of a person in front of him. This figure was shrouded by a shadow that allowed no detail to be seen. Yet despite the lack of sight, Jon somehow felt that *this* was the woman he had come to find, Dr. Susan Decker.

Yet, despite this impossibility, he knew he was no longer dreaming. This felt real. He could feel the oppressive chill of the stale air within the bridge. He could feel the twinge in his lungs from just having breathed through an oxygen mask on his journey here. He did not remember coming here, but he vividly remembered what Susan said to him within his fantasy.

Urging him.

Calling him.

Trying to concentrate – to *focus* – Jon's mind swirled

in a haze. He could only see the figure as Susan, now standing in front of him.

"Babe," he said with a tremble in his voice. "You're alive!"

He knew he should not believe his eyes. He'd *seen* her die at the hands of that creature. But he could not help succumbing.

Reaching out, this figure beckoned to him.

Without another thought, Jon rushed over, grabbing her in his tight embrace.

"Susan..." he said, relieved; his eyes tightly closed from happiness.

How can this be? he thought.

"You're alright. Everything'll be alright, I'm here now," he said.

Then slowly, as he embraced her, he began to feel that something was very, very wrong.

As he caressed the back of her head, he could not feel her hair. Instead, his hand touched a smooth undulating baldness. Something pulsing and covered in a thin slime.

Pushing himself back, he stared at what he had actually held in his arms; the animated corpse of one of the German crew members; a small man in a bloodied Richter Dynamics spacesuit, the front of which had been torn open, exposing a large cavity in this man's chest. The ribs had been broken outward, exposing the place where his internal organs should be, though they were now missing.

Burrowing into the back of its head, where Jon had placed his hand, thinking it was Susan, a dark spiny lifeform had dug in deep, and its tendrils sprouted out its back and coiled around the man's distorted face, each one wrapping around his features, leaving only the mouth and eyes exposed through bloodied gaps in the coil.

"Is something wrong, my love?" Though this corpse spoke in a heavily accented male voice, it still spoke words as if they were coming from Susan.

This was the last laugh of the creature that had controlled Jon's thoughts. It fooled him into believing he was safe aboard the Shenandoah, reunited with his love, instead of puppeteering him to the Frerichs.

Jon screamed in terror at this man staring at him with dead eyes. Staggering backward, Jon's eyes quickly caught sight of something within his periphery.

As he turned, he saw a line of a dozen bodies that hung upside down from the pipes overhead. This bridge had been turned into a human slaughterhouse.

Letting out a low, helpless moan, he fell to his knees, and saw that beneath these strung-up bodies, a pile of human remains lay. On top of this heap of body parts, he could see the real lips he had once kissed so dearly, attached to the lower remnants of a female head, the top of which was now ringed with gouges from an enormous mouth that had bitten into it.

This was what was left of Susan.

Within her remains, a multitude of black tendrils entwined around almost every part, working their way into her chunks of naked, decaying flesh.

"We apologise that we could not stand here in the flesh that you desired," the dead man said, still standing in the middle of the room facing Jon. The creature within its head then started to pulsate more rapidly, as a perverse grin crept up the dead man's face. "The time was too short, you see. And we were *so* hungry, and that flesh was *so* warm."

The man took a step forward, as the pulsating became like an audible heartbeat. "Soon, though," it said, almost out of breath. "*Soon that meat will rise.*"

A shrieking sound pierced the air, causing Jon to turn in shock. The last thing he saw was this creature-controlled cadaver advancing upon him in a monstrous fury. The dark lifeform swelling inside the skull now had its spines raised upwards in a twisted battle stance.

* * * * *

Dr. Wendy Oliver exited the elevator in a hurry and rushed down the corridor. She fought the rising panic within her as best she could. She had looked for Jon in every part of the ship she could think of – even looking within her *own* room – but she had found nothing. Not one single trace of him.

"Commander," she called out, approaching the medical bay, rapidly getting more out of breath.

As she strode into the room, she noticed Hofner sitting on the chair by her desk eating a sandwich. She then shifted her intense gaze to Davison.

"What's the matter?" the commander said, as he noticed the troubled concern etched into her face.

Hofner paid her arrival no attention and just continued to eat his snack, as if he was somehow oblivious to her entrance.

Beth and Bryce, both turned to Wendy, but Perkins did not. He continued staring at this uninvited guest, seemingly wondering his actual intentions.

"Commander," Wendy repeated, her breathing heavy. "Jon..."

"Is he okay?" Beth cut in.

"Gone." Wendy clarified. "He's gone. I can't find him."

"What?" Davison could only find that one word to say. He hated that things had gone from bad to worse since they had landed, or more correctly, *crashed* upon this moon. He was clearly losing patience with all the mounting bad fortune that seemed to be relentlessly piling on top of them, much like the falling rocks had done upon the Shenandoah. Yet, he was still determined that this would not be their graves as well.

"I looked everywhere," she panted. "And his EVA suit is gone. "

Davison closed his eyes as he processed this information.

Hofner was still eating, a smirk on his face.

Where would he go?" he asked Davison.

After a few beats, Beth thought aloud, "You think he went to the other ship?"

"He's definitely not on *this* ship?" Davison said to Wendy. "I'm not doubting what you're saying, but we-"

"I checked the airlock log. It was opened just over an hour ago." Wendy looked around at the people in the room. "That's gotta be him, unless any of you went and opened it?"

Everyone quickly fell quiet, until Davison spoke. "Alright, I guess we better see if we can find him. "

With a chuckle, Hofner stopped eating his sandwich and spoke quietly. "I'm afraid you have a slight problem with your plan. "

Davison, ignoring this, looked at Wendy. "Check the ship again, okay?" He turned to Beth. "And I need you to build that transmitter. "

"But-" she protested.

Hofner put down the remaining sandwich on a plate on the desk. "You do not have enough oxygen for this foolishness."

"Excuse me?" Perkins asked, but Hofner addressed only Davison in his reply.

"Before I made my presence known, I took the liberty of checking your air supply. There's simply not enough of it, at least not enough to waste on a full-scale search. There's just enough to refill your suits, and last maybe a few days here, as long as you shut off the majority of the ship."

"Is that true, Commander?" Perkins said.

"I have it in hand."Davison replied, frustrated at the German. "Now, Beth... The transmitter?"

"Mike, I can't-" she complained.

"I'm sorry but it's an order." He spoke sternly, the usual calm demeanor slipping. His tone was one he had never used with her before.

Beth glanced at Hofner and Davison before walking out of the room without saying another word.

When she was gone, Hofner stood. "There is, though, more than enough air to make a trip to my ship. And there, we have enough oxygen for a long time."

Davison couldn't help but notice that Hofner seemed to be enjoying their dire situation.

"We won't have to come back at all, you see?" the German continued. "We can go there. I can get the explosives, then we lure that beast outside and fly home, happy and healthy. You see, it will be lured. It won't be able to resist. It *wants* me. I am the *last* one left. I *escaped* it. Offended it by shrugging off its influences."

Davison shook his head. "Before we go off half-cocked, I know how we can get at least some oxygen to supplement our supply." He turned to Bryce. "You and Perkins get your suits on. I want you to take the sled over to the find, bring back the air tanks that you find there. I saw at least two on the floor, and one—"

"The tank from the dead man?" Perkins interrupted, hardly believing his ears. "Are you asking us to grave rob?"

"The dead have no use for them," Davison replied. "So why not?"

"Commander, I'm not okay with going out there," Perkins insisted. "And I'm certainly not okay going out there to steal from the dead. That's not only immoral, and unethical, but it's also against NTI regulations, and—"

Before Perkins could finish, Davison raised his hand up to silence him.

"If you don't mind," Hofner spoke up, "I'd like to go instead."

Davison raised a questioning eyebrow to this offer.

"I told you, you have misunderstood my intentions," Hofner continued. "I want to help. Besides, I know the place better than you all. I can go with Frau Bryce. Then when we come back with lots of oxygen, you can consider my plan, yes?"

Davison looked at Bryce to gauge her reaction.

"He knows if he steps out of line, I'll just put him down again," she said nonchalantly, unfazed by Hofner's offer.

Hofner smiled at her strangely. "Marvelous," he said. "We shall have much fun."

* * * * *

"You touch my ass again, and I'll remove your balls with a bullet," Bryce told Hofner, her weapon pointed at his crotch.

With a child-like laugh, he turned and walked out of

the Shenandoah's now open airlock. "I do like you Frau Bryce. Very much so. You are my kind of strong woman."

As she stepped out of the ship, she made sure to keep her aim on the German who stepped out onto the rocky terrain.

Around them, the air was still filled with thick poisonous mist as well as a haze of fine dust that fluttered down from the open rock above them, drifting down from the moon's surface.

Slamming her hand on the button to manually close the airlock, she turned and saw the German already walking away. She shouted after him, losing her patience. "I am not to be fucked with, Hofner. Wait for me!"

Without slowing, he glanced over his shoulder, tapped the side of his helmet, then said calmly, "No need to shout, mein liebling, I can hear you just fine over the radio."

As he turned back, she sighed, then stepped off the ship. She picked up her pace, and it was not long until she had caught up with Hofner.

"I think we are going to be *great* friends," he said, seeing her annoyed look.

She shook her head at him. "Can you stop saying shit like that?"

Soon, they disappeared from the sight of the ship, into the blanket of fog which hung thicker and deeper around the edges of the cavern.

On the Shenadoah's bridge, Beth pushed a motherboard back into the powered-down communications console. In front of her lay a collection of transistors, resistors, capacitors and chips that she had just removed and replaced.

Reaching forward, she flicked two switches upon the console that caused it to spring to life as it started its booting sequence. It made a series of high-pitched beeps, and lights over it flickered on and off.

"One moment," she said to Davison who sat another console with his back to her.

On her monitor, the screen displayed the words:

Secondary Unit - Status>Online

"Go ahead," she said, keeping her attention fixed on her monitor. "Try it now. "

Immediately Davison hit a button, but as he did, the console in front of Beth sparked and started to leak a dark smoke through the gaps where she had accessed the motherboard.

"Fuck sake, no!" she shouted. "Turn it off! Quickly!"

A low electric crackle emanated from her console as Davison pushed the button a second time, deactivating it.

He looked over his shoulder at the smoke spilling out around her. "No good, huh?"

After waiting for the smoke to clear, then ejecting the motherboard from its console, she slumped down in her seat and looked dejected.

Her demeanor changed as she caught a blinking light flashing fast beside her monitor from the corner of her eye.

She quickly reached for her headphones, pressed some commands into the computer, then listened intently.

"What is it?" Davison said, before raising his voice louder. "Beth?"

"Wait," she snapped as she concentrated on what she could hear in the headphones. After a few seconds she took them off and looked at Davison. "Someone's trying to contact us."

Davison looked at his own console. "There's nothing on my system."

The door to the bridge hissed open as Perkins walked in, as if on cue.

"It's on an EU assigned video phase," Beth said. "Only my system can receive those." She hit a few buttons. "Hang on. I'll send it to the monitor."

Davison stood up, then walked over to Beth, staring at the screen now filled with static.

"What's going on?" Perkins asked.

"Contact, it seems," Davison said, and they all stared at the monitor.

The static on screen began to clear as a weak image of Jon started to appear.

"Mics are hot," Beth said.

Despite Jon displaying his usual friendly smile, they all noticed that something was not right with him. His head appeared to be on a slight tilt, and from his neck, a bone appeared to bulge out and push against his skin from the inside.

"His eyes. What's wrong with..." Beth whispered, before trailing off.

Jon's eyes were indeed shocking, as they both appeared unnaturally milky.

"Could be the feed," Davison said under his breath, aware that Jon could hear them.

"I guess you didn't expect to see me again," Jon said on screen. His voice was slightly strained, but otherwise normal.

"Where the hell are you, Jon?" Davison said.

"You know where I am," he replied with a laugh.

"Are you all right, there?" Perkins asked. "What

about the organism on board?"

"The alien?" Jon asked, then answered with a shrug.

"Are you sure everything is okay?" Davison repeated the question.

Raising his hand into shot, Jon proffered a weakly clasped thumbs-up. "I'm better than alright," he said, his smile remaining. "I'm great in fact. I'm sorry I didn't tell anyone where I was going, but I knew you might not let me go."

"You're damn right about that," Davison said, smiling back at Jon, masking his feeling that none of this was as it seemed.

Dropping his hand, Jon asked, "How's your air holding out, anyway? There's plenty here. Enough for everyone."

"Did you find Susan?" Beth asked, changing the subject. Perkins shot her a quizzical look.

Jon appeared visibly upset by this question. As he slowly answered, he seemed to fight back the tears. "Commander, I don't know where Susan is. I searched the entire ship. No one's here. Not even any bodies. It's empty. Totally empty"

"And no creature at all?" Davison asked. "Nothing?"

Jon stopped in place for a few moments as he thought about the question. If it was not for the sound of his breathing, anyone might have considered that the screen had frozen.

Suddenly, Jon's face faltered, and Jon answered again, verbatim, his last sentence. "Commander, I don't know where Susan is. I searched the entire ship. No one's here. Not even any bodies. It's empty. Totally empty

Turning to Davison, oblivious to Jon's strange behavior, Perkins said, "That means it's safe to go over there! We don't have to worry. "

Leaning forward, Davison placed his hand over a small hole in the console, an inch beneath the monitor. Blocking this camera, he hid them from view as he turned to Perkins and whispered harshly in his ear. "Wise the fuck up and shut up. "

Perkins' expression dropped.

Davison continued to whisper. "I've known Jon for almost a decade. And that... *That* is not Jon. Something's wrong with him. He would *never* call me Commander. Ever."

"Commander?" Jon said over the speaker. "Is everything okay? I cannot see you?"

Removing his hand from the camera, Davison's expression changed back to a smiling one. "Sorry about that, Jonathan. Now, are you really okay? There seems to be something wrong with your neck?"

Twisting his head a little more to the camera, a crack of bone could be heard as Jon replied, "The airlock door was jammed so I had to force the auxiliary to open it. Must have pinched a nerve. Are you coming over?"

Davison glanced at Beth, who looked worried, then he turned back to the screen. "I dunno, Jonathan. Lots to consider. We will let you know. "

"Commander, this ship's ready to go," Jon insisted. "There are just a couple of circuits to fix, but nothing important. I can have it all done by the time you get here.'

"Okay. We'll talk it over, give us some time." Davison put his hand on Beth's shoulder to prompt her to cut the signal.

"Don't take too long, Commander," Jon said, his smile wide and forced. "I want to go home, don't you?"

As the monitor turned off, Beth looked up at

Davison. "He didn't even react!"

"I am missing something, obviously," Perkins said. "So he called you Commander? So what? He has just been through a very traumatic experience. Something we can all appreciate. "

"Wasn't just that. I called him Jonathan." Davison shook his head.

"And?" Perkins was very confused.

"His name isn't Jonathan," Beth said, looking at Perkins with a sad smile. "It's Jonas. "

The silence on the bridge was palpable as they all wondered what they had just seen. *Who* they had just seen.

The computer blinked off in front of Jon as the smile fell from his face, leaving only a blank and emotionless expression. His mouth hung slightly ajar. His eyes remained unblinking.

As his vacant expression remained, a squelching, suckling sound emanated from behind him, and a small trickle of blood ran from his nose.

There was another squelching sound, and Jon turned his head up straight.

Under the skin on Jon's neck, a tendril worked its way around from the inside, wrapped around the protruding neck bone, then pulled it back into place with a horrific *crack*.

Like the puppeteered figure he had met on this bridge, at Jon's back, lodged within the exposed cavity in the back of his head, a black spiny creature pulsed. Its tendrils spread deep into Jon's corpse – which was now under this monster's control.

* * * * *

Walking into the ruins of the Titan find, Bryce grabbed hold of a metal sled that lay on the ground outside a collapsed part of the excavation. Emblazoned with a large Richter Dynamics logo, she hit a button on the sled's controller, activating its hydraulic mechanism. Slowly, this sled lifted up from the dirt, then hovered a couple of inches from the ground, floating on top of a cushion of air that continuously pumped through the vents running around the sled's edges.

"This'll make things easier," she said aloud, looking from the sled to Hofner, who was now in front of a pile of rubble outside of the structure's main doorway. He was crouched down, removing chunks of rock from something hidden underneath.

As Bryce approached, pulling the sled, she saw that he was uncovering a buried body dressed in a Richter Dynamics spacesuit.

With a look of sadness, he turned to Bryce. "I tried to bury them as best I could. But I had little time. I could not bury everyone."

Glancing around, she noticed two other such piles of rubble nearby. Then, for the first time, she felt pity for this man. She had not realized until now the anguish he must have endured before arriving at the Shenandoah.

"I am sorry, my friend," Hoftner spoke to the body in German. "This is not the place for you. You are not anyone's butterflies."

After uncovering more of this body, Hofner turned it over then gingerly removed the oxygen canister from its backpack.

Handing it to Bryce, he then got to his feet and attempted to cover his grief with a smile.

Taking the canister, Bruce placed it on the sled behind her.

The German motioned into the structure's main doorway. "We can collect the American's oxygen from in there, then collect the ones from my other friends on the way out. "

Having left the sled at the entrance due to its size, Bryce and Hofner entered the doorway. Their flashlights joined with the blue glow from within these alien walls to light their way.

Bryce had forgotten the feeling she had experienced here, only a few hours ago; like she was standing within an ancient mausoleum. Though there might only be one body in the corridor, she felt the weight of death all around her. An unquantifiable gut feeling that rot and decay were as much a part of these walls, as the metal, wire, and bioluminescent light.

With her rifle now firmly in her hand, Bryce trod ahead carefully over the uneven ground as they approached the dead body of the American beside the cracked glass cylinder.

And though she expected to see the dead body as before, she saw that it was different.

That body was gone.

Instead, there was something else in its place.

Some*one* else.

Her eyes widened as she could not only see that the spacesuit was, like the missing body, American – but specifically belonged to the crew of the *Shaman* class starship, the Shenandoah.

Slicked in blood, this ripped space suit covered a female body, only the legs of which could be seen, as its top half was masked in the shadows behind the broken cylinder.

"Hofner! Here!" Bryce shouted as she slung her rifle over her shoulder then moved closer to the corpse. "It's one of ours!"

Shining her flashlight onto the upper torso of this body, Bryce gasped as the horribly mutilated body of Susan came into view. With no clothing from the waist up – her spacesuit torn to shreds above the belt line – she was nearly unrecognizable. Her flesh seemed butchered, then crudely reconstructed. Her chest displayed long, deep uneven gouges down its middle – as if it had been bifurcated in some primitive autopsy – before being haphazardly stuck back together with what looked like a thick, dark, oily substance. One of her breasts was also missing, as if it had been torn off then replaced with a mass of that same black substance.

The gouges did not only appear on her exposed chest; each of her arms also displayed a multitude that ran like dark wide fault lines across her otherwise pale flesh.

Moving her flashlight up, Bryce noticed yet another gouge that ran the width of the neck, then further up... her face— *Oh God, her face!*

Bryce felt cold sweat trickle down the small of her back as she saw that the top half of Susan's head was missing from the bridge of her nose, upward.

Hofner tried to see what Bryce stared at in horror, but the broken cylinder blocked his view. "What is it?" he said.

"It's," Bryce said, as she struggled to get the words out. "It's... Susan. *Our* Susan. "

Hofner's expression dropped. That was the woman he had seen slaughtered on his ship. Now she was somehow here at the excavation site? There was only one explanation.

"Stand back!" he shouted, "It's not what you think!"

Turning back to him in confusion, Bryce said "What are you talking about?" She did not see the smile appear on the lower half of Susan's massacred face. A cruel and malicious smile creeping up. The smile of a predator knowing that its prey had walked blindly into its trap.

Hofner backed up against the wall, his expression etched with fear. "Shoot it! Shoot it, quickly!"

Before Bryce could turn, Susan's corpse had reached up from the darkness, into Hofner's view.

Within the fleeting seconds before she grabbed Bryce and pulled her downward, this monstrous re-animation let out a terrifying screech from its lolling mouth.

Hofner launched himself forward, to grab Bryce and attempt to pull her out of the beast's grip. As he moved, his flashlight briefly illuminated a black, throbbing creature, dug deep within Susan's exposed cranium.

* * * * *

The rocks had again begun to fall upon the wreck of the Shenandoah. Most of its front section was almost completely consumed by this natural burial, and the rear was only half-consumed by the falling rocks, dust, and methane ice.

The airlock – just clear of this rising rock line – was closed. Davison, Wendy and Perkins all stood inside of it, their spacesuits on, ready to walk out.

With the inner door open, Beth – still in her jumpsuit – looked at them mournfully.

"I don't like this anymore than you do, Beth," Davison said.

Her face clearly expressed her trepidation for the entire plan.

"We can't wait any longer, despite it being blatantly obvious that there's something wrong at the site of the German ship. *And* with Jon. So, though I'd love to wait another three hours, we can't. We *have* to get more oxygen."

"I know," she replied.

"So wait here for Bryce and Hofner. We have to assume they're okay unless we find out otherwise. Keep the airlock clear of debris if you can. If it does get blocked, use the top hatch." Davison continued as he gave her a warm smile, "And please, keep trying that transmitter. You never know... Right?"

Wendy, carrying three rifles, handed one to Davison, who slung it over his shoulder, then handed one to Perkins, who took hold of it, examining it uneasily.

"I've never shot a gun before," he said, gripping onto the weapon awkwardly. "I don't think I *can*. "

"You don't take it, you don't come along," Davison said. "Can't have you defenseless out there. Simple as that."

"Don't worry," Wendy assured Perkins as he turned to her with a helpless expression on his face. "I'll teach you on the way. You'll be fine. "

With a soft, genuine tone in his voice, Perkins replied, "Thank you, Dr. Oliver. Thank you." He was used to being protected by others – his position at NTI demanded it. That was why Bryce had been assigned in the first place; to protect *him* as much as the mission itself. He was not, though, used to protecting himself.

Now Bryce was not here, and had turned against him in favor of the commander. Perkins would have no choice but to stop being passive - watching the world pass around him - and become an active participant.

Pressing the button on the control panel, Beth smiled as the inner door slid shut. Separating her and the rest of the crew.

"We'll call you from the Frerichs," Davison said to Beth through the intercom. "And take care of this beauty while we are gone. "

Through the glass, Beth smiled. "Are you talking to me or the Shenandoah?"

Glancing at her, Davison and Beth shared a look. A few seconds that said more than any words could; their unspoken bond clear as day within their gazes.

After the inner hatch was sealed and pressurized, the outer hatch opened. Perkins looked forward, out into the unforgiving atmosphere. The caverns under Titan's surface were a hellish landscape that he and his crewmates had no choice but to traverse.

As they exited the ship, Perkins prayed that he was dreaming. He would give anything to wake up in the comfort of his bedroom, deep in the heart of Neuvo Angeles.

Chapter Eight
Like Lambs…

The large metal door slid upwards, exposing the airlock hatch of the Richter Dynamics vessel. With each of them feeling a varying degree of fear, Perkins, Wendy and Davison exchanged wary glances as they slowly stepped into the hatch. With weapons in hand, Davison worried that this would not only be his last command decision, but his last decision of *any* kind.

His mind reeled with things they maybe *should* have done instead of coming here. They *should* have waited at the ship. They *should* have gone to the find site first. They *should* have brought more weapons. They *should*... They *should*... But all these *shoulds* did not change the fact the three of them stood at the precipice of a craft that, when they last were here, contained a murderous creature of unknown origin. And now, this craft contained a twisted version of Jon – Jonas – or something that looked like him.

As the outer doors closed behind them, the characteristic blasts of air jetted at them, purging the poisonous Titan fumes from within the chamber, and beginning the pressurization process.

Through the door's window into the ship, they could see the corridor stretching out in front of them. Dark. Foreboding. Unwelcoming.

Pressing themselves against the wall, hiding from anything that might be lying in wait, they were quiet as the inner door slowly hissed. Its heavy metal bulk then slid across, revealing the corridor.

With a raise of Davison's hand, Perkins and Wendy remained still as they listened out for any sign of trouble.

Taking a step out, Davison peered both ways down the corridor. He noticed a large smear of Susan's blood on the floor just outside the hatch. *This was a bad idea,* he thought, *a goddamn stupid, fucking bad, bad idea.*

The shadows in front of him moved.

Perkins jumped quickly back with a gasp, then aimed his rifle at the doorway. As he almost jammed his finger onto the trigger, he quickly paused as he saw that the thing that had just moved from the shadows to now stand in front of them, was not a monster, but was Jonas Fennell.

Still in shadow, but looking better, Jon smiled at the visitors. His eyes no longer looked milky but instead were their usual dark brown.

"Take it easy, for Christ's sake!" he said as he held up his hand.

Davison regarded him silently with an air of suspicion.

"I almost blew your face off!" Perkins snappe.

Wendy leaned over and nudged his rifle downwards, away from anyone.

"Nice to see you, too." Jon smiled, then waved them in. "Please. Come inside. Everything's fine. "

Cautiously, Davison led his other crewmates into the darkened corridor. The temperature of the ship felt significantly warmer than it had been during their last visit. As Davison removed his helmet then clipped it to his belt, he felt his body sweating within the spacesuit as he switched his flashlight off, relying instead on the emergency lighting onboard.

"Sorry 'bout the heat," Jon said without a further explanation

Following the Commander, Wendy and Perkins also removed their helmets, instantly feeling the discomfort of the heat.

Taking a step forward, Jon smiled at them as the light from the airlock caught his face, exposing the large bandage that adorned the back of his head.

"Come with me." He smiled. "I have something to show you."

Led by Jon, the crew entered a computer chamber.

Perkins' attention was on the surroundings, whereas Davison and Wendy were visibly more concerned with the man leading them.

"So, what happened to you?" Davison asked cautiously. "What happened to your head? It looks a bit more serious than just a pinched nerve."

Turning, Jon gave Davison an uneasy smile. "I was down in engineering and I was checking out one of the DKC units." He glanced around at them as he spoke. "I didn't realize it 'til later, but the damn Germans use caustic fluid in those things. I guess I got some of it on me. Hence..." He motioned to the bandage on his head.

"You got some fluid on your head, but not your hands or face?" Davison said suspiciously, his worry reinforced moment by moment.

Before Jon could answer, Wendy said, "I should really take a look at it. Make sure it's not too serious."

Without pausing, Jon replied, "In a little while. I've got more to do first."

As he turned to walk further into the room, Davison

shot Wendy a glance. She shrugged in answer to the silent question she understood all too clearly. *What was wrong with Jon?*

"It's too hot in here," Perkins said as he unzipped the front of his spacesuit.

"That's one thing I still have to fix. The temperature control unit has short-circuited." Jon faced his guests. "Now please, where are the others?"

"They're out, sourcing supplies," Davison replied, not wanting to go into detail. *Just in case,* he thought, though he was not sure in *what* case.

"If it is oxygen or food they are looking for, then they needn't have bothered. There's more than enough here, as I told you." Jon's voice was even, assured, calm. Things that Davison would never accuse Jon of being.

"Well, we can't tell them. Our radios can't cut through the RF. So Beth's waiting for them."

Having stepped to the side of the room with no one noticing, Perkins now stood next to a door with large lettering on it that read, *'Waffen'*. A word that Perkins knew to mean that beyond this door was the ship's weapons cache. Pressing the button to open it, Perkins frowned when nothing happened. He called back to Jon. "Why won't this door open?"

Turning his head with a jolt and a large smile, Jon answered without a moment's pause, cutting into his conversation with Davison without any notice. "Must be a fuse. We should go down to engineering to see what we can do."

Feeling this growing sense of unease, Davison caught Jon's attention. "Jon, you better let Wendy take a look at your head. That coupler fluid can cause a nasty scar, maybe worse."

Jon looked at Wendy, then back to Davison. "Okay," Jon said nodding. "She can come with me to engineering – it's where I took the medical supplies to fix myself up. We need to hurry, though. We should leave this Moon as soon as possible, shouldn't we?"

Davison glanced at Wendy, who nodded. "I'll be okay," she said, as she motioned down at the rifle in her hands, signaling that she had adequate protection with her.

"And what about the extra-terrestrial?" Perkins said, and for the first time, Davison was thinking the exact same thing. "How can you be sure it's not waiting around the next corner for us?"

With his smile turning to a rictus grin, Jon replied, "If there *was* a monster here, why am I still breathing and walking around the ship freely? Shouldn't I, too, be dead?"

"Let's go check your head," Wendy cut in, motioning Jon toward the exit.

With a nod, he replied, "After you, *please.* "

"She doesn't know where she's going, Jonathan," Davison said. He was poking around for more reactions to the incorrect name; while simultaneously ensuring that Wendy was in a protected position.

"Very good point, Commander," Jon replied as he moved to the exit, Wendy in tow; her finger surreptitiously ready on her weapon's trigger.

"And please," Jon said before disappearing into the next room. "It's Jonas, not Jonathan. "

Shooting a glance to Perkins, Davison immediately doubted everything he had felt. He could very well be wrong.

Maybe nothing was untoward here? Maybe Jon was fine?

"You know what I see as a bit strange?" Perkins proffered as he turned to look to the empty doorway.

"That he doesn't seem phased by any of this?" Davison guessed.

Perkins nodded. "It's as though he's forgotten all about Dr. Decker. "

Davison was surprised at Perkins' apparent concern, which was soon quashed when Perkins said, "Guess he didn't like her all that much. "

With a sigh, Davison did not address the comment, and instead said, "I think you and I should do our own inspection of the ship. "

"Shouldn't we first try to open the door to the armory?" Perkins said as he motioned to the door across the room.

Without giving Perkins any time to protest, Davison said, "First things first." then walked toward the corridor. "We can get in there where we know what we are up against."

"I think there's something I should tell you," Wendy said as she followed Jon down the corridor, her rifle tight in her hands.

The heat within this lower level was more intense. Though, despite her discomfort, her eyes did not leave the back of Jon's head.

"What should you tell me?" Jon asked without looking back.

The emergency lighting that ran along the ceiling cast its faint glow upon his head, illuminating a dark stain beneath.

"Well," she said. "I'm not what you think I am. "

Unseen by Wendy, a wry smile pulled at the corners

of Jon's mouth.

She continued, "I've got a confession to make. You see I'm not really a regular doctor. "

"Then what kind of doctor are you?"

"I'm not a general practitioner at all. I'm bio-physics. They just hired me on this mission as I had a medical degree. They didn't care about the discipline."

"Bio-physics?" he mused. "Fascinating."

"I'm more or less the same kind of doctor as Susan." Her words were chosen carefully. She wanted a reaction from Jon. *Any* reaction. Something human.

"Why are you telling me this?" Jon asked as he stopped at a closed door with the word *'Maschinenbau'* written upon it. Turning to her, with his grin still in place, he waited for an answer.

"No reason. Just sayin'," she lied. Her medical discipline was the study of biological phenomena, and at the moment she had a greater feeling that something was wrong with Jon. Something that must be biological in nature. No matter if his eyes seemed fine now, or if he had an answer for everything, he was acting very unlike himself. The same way she had seen people act with fungal infections of the brain. The kind of infection the miners on Mars had contracted after prolonged exposure to ancient spores. All the crew should have had their vaccinations against these kinds of infections before they left earth, but who knew if Jon had?

"You know, I have a secret of my own, too," Jon said with a smile, as he pushed the button on the door frame.

The door slid open, exposing pitch blackness inside. A thick blanket of heat poured out, hitting Wendy, and making her feel slightly nauseous.

Before he could finish his thought, Jon walked into

the dark room. "I just need to turn the lights on first," he called out.

Wendy could not see within the room. The dim corridor light barely broke past the door jamb. Inside though, she could smell something awful. Something thick and metallic.

She waited.

The only noises she could hear were the shallow breaths coming from her own lungs, and the low electrical buzz from the corridor's lights.

As she tried to focus inside, Wendy felt like she was being watched.

"Jon?" she said with a tinge of worry in her voice. "Jon?"

After a beat, his voice came from within the thick shadows in the room. "Come on in. It'll just take me another second or so. "

Swallowing hard, she gripped her weapon a little tighter, and then against her better judgment, she took a step inside.

A lone silhouette against the dim light from the corridor, Wendy paused a few feet into the darkness as she convinced herself that this was a bad idea.

Before she could walk back, the door behind her slid shut. As the metal of the door connected with the frame, it let out a deep clank that echoed within the room. It hung in the darkness for a moment before dissipating.

The room's window let in a minute amount of the light from the corridor. Not enough to illuminate much.

"Jon," she said again, as she tried to steel her nerves. With one hand she reached back to the helmet clipped to her belt, looking to activate the communication button on its side.

Before she could find it, a soft clatter of metal emanated from the other end of the room.

"Jon, answer me, damnit!" she said as she then gripped her rifle with both hands. "What the hell are you doing?"

Raising her weapon slowly, she tried to discern anything around her, but her eyes could not adjust fast enough to the thickness of the room's shadows. She was effectively blind, only able to see vague shapes on a darker background.

Another soft clatter, this time like the sound of a wooden wind chime clanging together in a soft breeze. It came from in front of her. *Directly* in front of her.

Wendy turned back in the direction of the door, but before she could take another step, she froze in place.

The vague shape of something large and dark stood in her way, directly in front of her escape. Silhouetted in the glow through the window.

Blinking hard, she tried to focus her eyes.

"Please Jon," she said, taking a few steps back, away from this shape in front of her. "You're scaring me..."

Was her mind playing tricks on her? Was there a spore infection that Jon had passed to her, that was maybe resistant to her vaccinations? Was the shape in the door nothing but her imagination?

As she retreated from the shape in a panic, her back collided with something solid. something that made more of the chiming sound. In an instant, she remembered her suit's flashlight. Cursing herself for not doing so sooner, she released one hand from her rifle and found its *on* switch.

As the flashlight sprung to life, the beam shot out and over the chiming object.

She gasped, startled.

She was face to face with one of the dead German astronauts. A woman who hung upside down from the pipes along the ceiling. Her body swung from its impact with Wendy, the chains holding it up rattled lightly, making that familiar chiming sound.

Wendy screamed. She twisted around, but before she could escape, something grabbed her by the helmet on her belt and pulled her backward with tremendous force. As her arms flailed, she dropped her weapon, and soon found herself deeper in the room – surrounded by many more hanging bodies; all of them like the first, and those on the bridge hung upside down from the ceiling. All, very dead. All, very decayed. The smell in the room - their congealed blood, and heated flesh - was suddenly unbearable.

In a fit, she wrenched herself loose from whatever had hold of her and pushed her way free from the confines of the surrounding corpses.

As she bolted for the door again, her flashlight briefly illuminated the shape that had stood in her way. It was Jon, bearing a malicious, hungry expression. Drool dripped from his lips like a starved hyena.

Before she could react, Jon lunged, grabbed her arm, and dragged her toward him again.

As her flashlight traced his face, she saw his pupils more closely.

The light shone brightly into his face, and small black tendrils that had mocked an iris by creating a spiral over Jon's eyeball shot outward; reacting angrily to the illumination. Jon let out an animalistic screech.

Desperate to get away, Wendy clawed at Jon's face. She knew in her mind that this was no longer the man she had known. This was *not* a simple fungal infection. Whatever this was, it meant her harm.

As her fingers raked his cheek, Jon's skin came off under her nails, like a warm knife through wet clay. As his cheek tore open, Jon's sinew and bone were exposed; the sinew and bone wrapped in thin black tendrils.

Jon's mouth frothed with green bile as his screeches got louder and his grip grew tighter.

Spinning her around, he pulled hard on her hair, then held her in front of him like an offering to some unseen god. Caught in his vice-like grip, she tried to break free, but he was too strong. *It* was too strong.

The flashlight beam waved madly in front of her, as something within the hanging corpses moved out from the shadows. A large mass from within the shadows of the bodies began to unfold itself from the ceiling, then leapt heavily to the floor.

In a horrifying apparition of death, the creature that had felled Susan now approached slowly. It winced slightly when the light hit its dark flesh.

Like the predator meeting its prey, it regarded her closely with every step. And then, Wendy was face to face with death itself.

With his rifle held close and waist-high, Davison remained on guard as he and Perkins walked slowly down a lower-level corridor. Sweat droplets decorated their faces as the heat in these lower levels grew more and more suffocating the further down they ventured.

Unlike Davison's experienced grasp, Perkins held his weapon more gingerly, as he pretended to know how to work a firearm – trying to convincing himself as much as Davison. As he trailed behind, he glanced up at the reduced glare of the overhead light, wishing for their luck to somehow change.

"It's another level down," Davison said as he motioned to a small flight of metal stairs to the right of them.

"It's going to be even hotter down there, isn't it?" Perkins grimaced.

Davison nodded, and began descending the stairs. "Unfortunately, yes," he said. He suddenly halted on the stairs. His eyes narrowed as he turned to Perkins with a confused look.

"What's the matter?" Perkins asked.

"Think about it," he replied. "We're sweating here like champs, since we got on this ship, right?"

"And?"

"And Jon wasn't sweating *at all*, was he?"

"You're casting doubt on Jon Fennell, again? But he *knew* his name. We have checked a lot of this ship. There are no monsters that *I* can see, just as he said. Or am I again missing something only you can see?"

"Well, we haven't checked the whole ship." Davison began to descend again. "Look, we better hurry, engineering *has* to be close."

As they reached the bottom of the stairs, the corridor in front of them split in two directions. Both seemingly identical to each other. No sign of what lay down either path.

"We better split up," Davison said, turning to Perkins. "You think there are no monsters, so you shouldn't have a problem with that, right?"

"Right," Perkins replied, never willing to admit any weakness.

"Go that way," Davison said as he motioned to the

left. Then, pointing to the right, said, "I'll go down here. "

Perkins smiled a thin smile.

"If you see anything, contact me, okay?"

After a few minutes of defensively walking down the murky corridor, Davison came up to a door labeled, *'Maschinenbau'*. He had given up trying to decipher the foreign language a few minutes after they began this search. He decided instead to just open every door he passed, looking in for any danger or preferably a friendly face.

Looking in the window of the door, he couldn't see anything through the darkness. As his hand reached out for the button, a sickening, muffled scream echoed from within the room.

Without a moment's pause, Davison reached forward and slammed the button. He swung his rifle up and leveled it at the opening door. As the door slid open, he peered briefly into the darkness within the room before moving cautiously inside. He wavered as the rising heat hit him, along with the foul smell. He tried to focus. He realised that he could not even tell the size of the room.

Before he could reach for his flashlight, another sound caught his attention; a low moan to his right. Quickly he grabbed the light, switched it on, then turned his rifle's aim toward the noise.

As the light's beam moved, it lit a terrible vision; the dark shape of the enormous, chitinous jaw biting into the throat of Dr. Wendy Oliver. She tried to scream as blood spurted down the front of her jumpsuit. Her face was chalk-white and her eyes rolled back into her head.

When the light hit the enormous creature, it squealed and dropped her body, then clambered noisily into the darkest shadows of the room.

As her body hit the floor, Wendy landed in a seated position in the opposite Davison. When she landed, her head lolled backward so far it hit her back, facing him whilst upside down. With her chewed-out throat now exposed wide, her neck spurted blood in an arc upward as her head clung onto her body by only a thin amount of skin and sinew.

Feeling sick, Davison turned and aimed at where the creature had retreated. Suddenly, from behind, the living corpse that was Jon Fennel smashed into Davison, knocking the weapon from his grasp.

Grabbing his commander's head, Jon flung Davison with incredible ease across the floor and into the seated remains of Wendy.

As Davison collided with her near-decapitated corpse, her body slumped backward on top of him. Her grotesquely exposed throat fell down over his screaming face, covering him in a warm spray of arterial blood, spraying his mouth with her gore.

Before he could escape the weight of her remains, he felt a sharp pain as Jon gripped his ankle tightly, then dragged him out and swung him through the air like a rag doll; tossing him across the room with ease.

Davison landed with a painful thud by the still-open door.

As he opened his blood-smeared eyes, Davison felt his body ache and he quickly blinked away the redness of the remnants of Wendy's blood in his eyes.

Managing to glimpse his rifle, lying only a few feet away, he kicked out his heel to try and catch the end of it.

As his shoe connected with the weapon's hilt, the jolt of his flashlight caught sight of Jon speeding towards him on all fours.

With the bandages hanging loose from Jon's head, a thick black oil dripped from his open cranium - revealing the edges of the pulsing creature dwelling within its cavity. Jon's mouth opened unnaturally wide as he screeched in fury.

Jumping on top of Davison, Jon continued screeching as he lowered his deformed maw, ready to bite.

Before his teeth could make contact with Davison's face, a gunshot rang out.

A bullet collided with Jon's neck, exploding out from the other side, sending him tumbling sideways across the floor.

Davison turned with shock, and for the first time was relieved to see Perkins, standing in the doorway, nervously holding his smoking gun.

A throaty gurgling sound came from Jon as his body contorted on the floor in pain, emitting a pitiful cry. Perkins grimaced at that grotesque sight, and Davison quickly scrambled to his feet, took hold of his own rifle, then turned it on the writhing Jon.

He pulled the trigger, and the shot collided with Jon's head, smashing it inward. His already broken skull collapsed into the black creature within.

The cries from Jon's mouth were cut off immediately.

As Davison looked up from Jon's remains, he slowly backed toward Perkins at the doorway. "Thanks," he said as his voice trembled.

"That's okay. I heard a scream, so..."

"That thing..." Davison said quietly. "That *creature* was here. It went to the end of the room. "

"Really? Is it still here?"

Davison's flashlight scanned the room, and the beam landed on the German corpses that swayed from the ceiling.

"Oh my God," Perkins said.

"Come on," Davison said as he retreated into the hallway. "We've gotta warn the others."

Chapter Nine
...To The Slaughter

Back on the Shenandoah, Beth sat at her console, soldering iron in her hand. Her work on the KFM transmitter was just a constant repeat of trial and error. Eleven trials and eleven errors, to be exact.

A small pile of burnt-out resistors sat on the desk next to her.

She concentrated hard on the work at hand.

Outside, a large, sharp rock made of ice fell from the roof of the cavern, plummeting down onto the ship below. As it collided with the Shenandoah's hull, it smashed through its metal chassis and into a large mass of wires and conduits, sending sparks exploding outward like fireworks.

Onboard, as the collision boomed throughout the ship's interior, the dim lighting suddenly cut out, leaving only the bridge's console lights illuminated.

"Shit," Beth said, as she checked gauges on her screen, then tried flicking a few switches.

She grunted when the switches did nothing.

Slowly, she closed her eyes as she took deep, calming breaths.

She did not want to go outside, but had no choice.

In the corridor outside the airlock, Beth stood in her spacesuit – helmet locked in place.

With a fearful look in her eyes, she took a few more

deep breaths before she put her hand up to the door's release button.

Pausing, she suddenly realized that she had left her tools on the bridge.

"Fuck. Fucking dumbass, Sladen. "

As she walked back to the bridge, muttering, she did not see the outside door of the airlock begin to open.

After setting her helmet down onto the console, Beth crouched and pulled out a small aluminum toolbox from underneath.

The sound of a nearby door opening echoed through the bridge's open door, followed by the same hissing sound of the door closing.

Standing slowly, Beth called out, "Bryce? That you?"

Cautiously moving to the doorway, she peered out.

Waiting quietly, she listened for the slightest new sound. The ship had been otherwise silent; the only sound being the low noise of the half-powered bulbs, mixed with the occasional clank of rocks hitting from the outside.

No other sounds were forthcoming, so Beth turned back into the bridge, and picked up her tools and helmet.

As she turned back to the airlock, she suddenly came face to face with Hofner, who had been standing less than a foot behind her.

Like a ghastly apparition, he stared blankly through his broken helmet. With its face plate cracked, its glass had shattered inward and splintered into many parts of the German's face. Shards embedded deep into many parts of his face, and a sliver of glass had split his left eye in two. The other eye, still whole, was a milky white, and didn't blink.

The rest of his suit was a torn mess of blood, plastic,

and fabric.

Horrified, Beth was too shocked to scream as she backed up against her console.

With sluggishly dragged footsteps, Hofner advanced on her. His mouth hung open as though trying to speak, yet only a weak sigh escaped his lips.

As her back hit the console Beth realised she had retreated as far back as she could go. Before being able to escape his advance, she noticed what he held in his hand; a black pulsing mass that throbbed within his grip. He raised it up toward her.

The hissing sigh from his mouth became a moan, then a slur of words, "Take…. us..." he said, salivating through the dripping blood and broken glass embedded in his mouth.

As he pushed the squirming creature outward, she gripped the toolbox in her hand, and swung it through the air.

Crashing into the side of his helmet, the force of the toolbox's blow sent Hofner to the floor.

With no time to feel any semblance of victory, Beth could only stare in shock as Hofner clambered back to his feet almost immediately.

Darting to the side, Beth made a beeline for the door. As she moved, Hofner reached out to grab her, narrowly missing her as she sprinted from the bridge and down the dark corridor.

She continued to move at full speed, down the half-dozen levels of the ship. Thinking of nothing except escaping the man she could hear loudly chasing her, wailing in rage. She could tell from the growing loudness of his roars that Hofner was no longer shambling slowly, but instead was running at speed.

Hofner's angry screeches echoed around her as she flung herself into the open airlock hatch. Rushing to the console inside, she slammed her fist on the button to close its inner door.

As the hydraulics sounded, Hofner appeared in the doorway. He let out an angry growl as the large metal slab slid onto him. He braced himself between the door and its frame.

She gasped as she could see that, in his hand, he still carried the black creature. And in the brighter light of the airlock, she could see it much more clearly. As she stared, its long, thin tendrils reached out hungrily toward her.

Exerting an immense strength, Hofner stopped the inner door in its tracks, a loud hydraulic screech sounding in the walls as it fought to close.

Beth turned to the console. She jabbed the main door button repeatedly, as she simultaneously held down two smaller buttons below.

The console beeped as the screen went red, displaying the words:

Pressurization Aborted.
Outer Hatch Override Enabled.

Stuck between the door and the frame, Hofner then screeched louder as he pushed harder against the metal. Its mechanism seized loudly and furiously, as it started to lose the battle.

The airlock loosed a loud alarm, as the manual override forced the outer door to slide open.

A blast of air from the outside shot in through the opening door, then pulled at Beth. She raced out the door as she struggled to put on and lock her helmet in time.

Behind her, Hofner had managed to open the door wider.

As the outside atmosphere dragged Beth outside, she frantically finished securing her helmet. As the poisonous air and deadly pressure flooded her lungs, she twisted the lock around her neck. Her eyes darted to the attached air hose, which was not connected to her suit.

As the caustic fumes engulfed her, their toxicity quickly attacked; not to mention the deep cold that plunged her body into a tortuous cold.

Sinking to the ground, blood trickled from her nose, her eyes, ears, and mouth.

Her skin lost all its color as the beginning stages of frostbite grayed her.

Mustering all of her remaining energy, she managed to connect the air tube to her suit. As she did, the suit automatically sealed itself and its life support system kicked in.

Beth gasped frantically as the suit's oxygen battled the poisonous fumes in her lungs. Managing to glance toward the airlock, Beth could see Hofner breaking free of the inner door, then clambering outside.

With maximum effort - with her body screaming at her to stop - Beth got to her feet, and ran as fast as she could.

The blood in her body felt like it was on fire, and her heart painfully pushed it through her veins. Every part of her body ached.

Beth could not remember how long she ran for, nor how far she had travelled. All she knew was the searing pain she was still in. The pain that Titan's atmosphere had inflicted in her.

Coming to the end of another cavern, she slowed down and turned around, half-expecting to see Hofner standing directly behind her, with that creature still in his - its - hand.

But Hofner was not there.

All she could see was the darkness of this catacomb-like cave system, intermittently illuminated by lightning from above the cracked surface. Her flashlight provided very little, yet welcome, light through the darkness in front of her.

Staggering forward, she continued her journey, her flashlight's beam dancing up and down with each step, throwing its light in a continual rhythm across her path.

Each lightning flash that pulsed from the cracks high above illuminated the surrounding expanse with an almost strobe-like effect.

At first that was all there was.

But soon, Beth's pursuer appeared on the horizon, far behind her, his presence only silhouetted within each flash of lightning from the surface.

And, at every explosion from within the Forseti crater, his figure appeared closer than before.

Unaware of his approach, Beth staggered on as fast as her body would allow.

All she wanted was rest.

A lightning flash. He was nearer.

All she wanted was to fly away from here.

Another flash. He was almost behind her.

All she wanted was—

Hofner grabbed Beth's shoulder, yanking her backward to the ground. As she fell, she stared up, and saw the lightning flashes expose his visage. They highlighted the monstrous scowl adorning his glass-pierced face, now bearing down on her.

Her screams reverberated across this cavern, their echoes dancing across the uninviting vista. Her tormented cries were matched only in volume by the ferocious, bestial wails of her attacker.

Standing on the bridge of the SMS Frerichs, Perkins was guarding the open door nervously. He gripped his weapon close to his chest.

Between his glances into the half-lit corridor and back at Davison – now sitting at a console – Perkins kept staring at the hanging chains, dangling from the ceiling above the mass of blood and black liquid across the other side of the room. The strung-up bodies and pile of flesh no longer there.

Perkins was equally worried that guarding this door might not be enough, should the creature decide to attack from above.

As Perkins panicked about every thought he had, he could hear his pulse beating loudly in his ears. As if his body was trying to communicate. Trying to tell him to move. To run. To not stand in harm's way.

"Shenandoah..." Davison spoke clearly into a microphone. "Shenandoah..." His voice was tired, his eyes closed. "Come in." His voice began to crack as he pleaded, "Beth, please answer." He had been trying to reach the ship for the last ten minutes, to no avail. Nothing answered but static.

Shaking his head mournfully, he said to Perkins. "I don't know what else we can do. "

After quickly checking the corridor again, Perkins snapped, "Let's get the hell out of here, then." Realizing his harsh tone, he put on a smile, and continued softly, "Bryce and the German must have gone back by now. They are probably on their way here as we sit panicking. That's why the radio can't raise them. They are not there."

Davison thought about his theory, then looked back at the radio.

Perkins continued, "If we go now, we can meet them halfway, then we can all come back together. En masse. Safety in numbers and all that. Besides, it will give us time to plan properly. Especially as we now know more than we did before."

"Shenandoah... come in. Beth?" Davison pleaded into the microphone.

"We can figure this out later, Michael," Perkins said, hoping the informality of using the commander's first name would curry some favor.

Reluctantly, Davison stood up from his seat, then grabbed his gun that had been propped against the communications console.

"I swear to you, the oxygen canisters *were* here," Perkins said as he and Davison stared at the empty racks next to the airlock. All the spare suits that *had* been there, complete with oxygen packs, were now gone. All that remained was a crushed helmet that lay in the middle of the floor.

"And the suits?" Perkins continued. "There was a full rack of them, correct? Or am I going mad here?"

"We should check these," Davison said, walking to the row of lockers along the other side of the wall.

Opening the locker doors, the men soon found that each one was the same as the last; empty.

"It wants to keep us here," Davison said.

Perkins thought for a moment, and he felt a chill trickle down his spine. "Then again, this could have been Hofner. Playing us. Trapping us with that *thing*."

As Davison heard those words, he knew it was the more likely explanation,

"There must be something else we can use to get outside," Perkins said. "Maybe there's some emergency suits somewhere else on the ship?"

"Do *you* want to go looking for them?" Davison replied. Perkins said nothing, "Me neither." Then, checking the small display on his spacesuit arm, Davison said, "Seems I got twenty minutes of oxygen left." He motioned to Perkins to check his display. "What's yours saying?"

Perkins checked, then shook his head. He had none left.

"Let's get back to the bridge. Barricade the door until we know more. We'll have more control of the situation from there and can start the checks of what we need to do to get this ship into the sky. "

Less than ten minutes later Davison tried to hail his ship again from the bridge.

"Shenandoah? Come in. If you can hear this but can't reply, know that we are on the bridge. We do not know the creature's location, so we have barricaded ourselves in this room. "

"Shhhh." Perkins said.

Davison stopped and looked up at Perkins, now standing at the observation window, staring, wide-eyed, down onto the surface outside. Without looking back, Perkins whispered, "Somebody's out there!"

Davison hurried across the bridge to the long

window at the end of the room. Standing beside Perkins he, too, stared at the ground, which sat over fifty feet beneath them.

Davison saw nothing.

"I saw them a second ago," Perkins continued whispering. "I did. I think..."

They stared for a few moments, until Perkins pointed a finger and said, "There!"

They both watched as they saw a figure in an NTI spacesuit emerge from the thick mist.

Staggering, this figure protectively held an arm over its ribs as it repeatedly glanced back over its shoulder.

"Is that Beth?" Davison asked with hope.

Perkins' tone was not so hopeful, "There's somebody behind her."

As a red light flashed on Beth's arm's display, it read in large lettering:

EMERGENCY -> Reserve air depleted.

Her helmet's faceplate dripped with blood that streaked the outside of the glass.

She could barely see the SMS Frerichs as it loomed up high in front of her.

Behind, Hofner appeared through the fog, closing in on her with a terrifying roar.

With the wounds from the glass in his face, as well as the burning atmosphere on his skin, Hofner would have already been a horrific sight. But After Beth escaping his grasp smashing her helmet repeatedly into his exposed face, he was now almost unrecognizable. Beneath the splayed-out broken helmet, his face was a mashed pulp with one eye glaring wickedly out from the gore. Protruding from the bloody mess, a few dozen black tendrils flailed wildly, trying to reconstruct what had been destroyed beyond recognition.

Running down the corridor, both men holding their guns, Perkins shouted after Davison, "What are you going to do?"

When Davison did not answer, Perkins caught up and grabbed him by the arm, pulling him to a stop. Moving himself into the commander's path, he pleaded, "You can't let them in! They might be like Fennel." He had trouble speaking his next words, so they came out strangled. "We could all wind up dead."

"If you think I'm going to leave Beth out there, just see what happens when you try and stop me. "

With only a few feet to go until she reached the airlock, Beth collapsed to the ground. Her strength was as exhausted as her air supply. Her breathing whined as she gasped for any air from within the empty canister.

Behind her, Hofner approached; gleeful at his prey's collapse.

From outside the inner door, with his eyes focused through the window to the outer airlock, Davison slammed the button on the control panel. As the cycle to open this airlock began, the hatch filled with plumes of air as the compression started.

Impatiently, and impossibly, Davison willed for the process to speed up.

Arriving at his side, Perkins looked from the glass to the pressurizing room, then to the commander. "Are you sure about this?" he asked nervously.

Cutting off any hope that Perkins would get an answer, a beeping sounded loudly as the outer airlock doors opened. For a moment, the two men could only see the dingy, fog-filtered light from Titan seeping into the exposed hatch.

"Come on, come on," Davison prayed aloud.

Perkins' eyes widened as they both saw Hofner, dressed in his Richter Dynamics spacesuit, dragging the NTI astronaut through the doorway, his back facing them.

"It's Beth," Davison said under his breath, as he saw the name patch stating 'Sladen' on the breast of her s uit.

When Hofner and Beth were inside the hatch, Davison activated the closing of the airlock. The usual hissing began as the moon's air was quickly purged out of the hatch, and replaced with oxygen.

Davison waited for the depressurization and then for the inside door to open.

"Why isn't he turning?" Perkins asked as he watched Hofner stand upright in front of Beth, looking to the outer door.

After a few moments, the door alarm sounded, the light above flicked green and the inner door slid away.

Rushing in, Davison kneeled beside Beth. He looked stunned at the blood that coated her helmet, then as he saw her gasping for air inside, still trapped within the sealed oxygenless suit. He reached down with speed, twisted the airtight collar ring, and removed her helmet as quickly as he could.

She coughed as the oxygen rushed back into her lungs. The blood that had trickled out of each facial orifice when she was outside the Shenandoah was now just dried red lines.

"Talk to me," Davison said in a panic. "Are you okay?"

Her eyes opened wide, and she stared upward as she tried to speak. Her expression grew more and more terrified.

Following her line of sight, Davison finally looked up, directly into the grotesque, decimated face of what was once Hans Rudi Hofner. In this bright light, the glass shards embedded in his face reflected the light like the sun hitting the sea on a bright day. With Hofner's heart having long since stopped, there was no pumping blood to mask his wounds anymore. His fog-burned, dried-up, massacred visage was gruesomely clear, made more terrifying under the airlock's neon glow that now illuminated it.

Before Davison could scramble to his feet, Hofner yanked him upward by his throat.

Beth could only lay there helplessly, looking on.

Lashing out with his fists, Davison punched the side of Hofner's head, causing the remnants of his helmet to snap off. Fully exposing the damage to his skull.

Standing by the door, Perkins witnessed the attack. As before, he lifted his weapon, pointed it at Hofner, and fired.

The weapon shot with a tremendous blast, the sound deafening in the close quarters. The gunshot collided with the side of Hofner's belly, causing him to drop Davison, and slam against the opposite wall.

Choking, Davison scrambled backward to Beth.

Hofner, though, was only temporarily subdued. With black bile now cascading from his lacerated and broken mouth, he turned and roared at Perkins as he stood up straight. From his new wound, some of his entrails forced their way out, but the undead German paid them no mind.

Facing away from Davison, without a helmet to hide the back of his head, Hofner's parasite could be seen clearly. With the rear of his skull missing, the black mass pulsed furiously from within as it controlled Hofner in totality, and forced his corpse to barrel toward Perkins.

Davison could only gape at the monster as it grabbed Perkins by the face, lifted him a foot clear from the floor, then slammed him into the metal wall of the hatch with a loud growl.

The back of Perkin's head made a small cracking sound as his skull collided with the wall's solid surface. His eyes rolled up into his head, and his attacker then pushed its hand harder into Perkin's face.

Perkins – petrified, and in agony – stared out through the fingers of his attacker's hand, watching as the German's mutilated face roared in bestial fury.

Suddenly there was a sickeningly wet wrenching sound in his ears. Perkins presumed it was the sound of his own head caving in, but just then, the pressure on his face diminished and he fell to the floor. Looking up through the pain, he watched as Hofner staggered backward, letting out a terrible hissing cry, then collapsed motionless into a twisted heap.

Next to him, Davison, his breath heavy, held the black parasite, freshly ripped out of Hofner's exposed cranium.

After a beat, Davison threw this pulsing monstrosity to the floor, then crushed it under a heavy boot. Reaching behind his own head, Perkins felt the wet sticky patch in his hair. He winced as his nerves screamed in pain at the touch.

"Are you okay to walk?" Davison asked, lowering down on his haunches. He had a look of genuine concern on his face.

Perkins nodded.

Then Davison turned to Beth. He touched her face gently.

"How are we going to win this?" Perkins asked. "This was just one tiny thing, and it nearly destroyed me."

Davison turned, and with a bitter smile, he said, "He may have been a strange sonofabitch, but Hofner had a plan. We just gotta lure that thing out, then destroy it. "

Chapter Ten
The Trap

Perkins held a wad of tissue to the back of his throbbing skull as he yet again stood by the door to the bridge; back in his previous look-out post.

He removed the dressing from his head and took a look at it. *Thank God, the bleeding stopped,* he thought, seeing no new blood on the tissue. The last thing this situation needed was any one of them to be a dead weight. There would hopefully be plenty of time to rest soon, but now was not the time to be a coward and play on his injury for sympathy. for sympathy. He watched as Davison interrogated Beth, trying to make sense of the events. He watched as Davison interrogated Beth, trying to make sense of the events.

Nearby, at the first console, Beth sat upright in a chair. She glanced emptily at the black and red stained floor in front of her, clearly trying to come to grips with the situation. Davison had told her about Jon's fate, which just added to her feeling of claustrophobia. She felt as if all the walls were closing in on her, inch by inch.

Davison sat next to her with a look of concern on his face. "So, Hofner showed up at the Shenandoah... then what?" he prompted.

She swallowed painfully, the effects from her exposure to Titan's atmosphere having left a lasting, agonizing impression.

"He had one of those small, horrible creatures with him," she replied, her voice hoarse. She shuddered at the memory. "I managed to crush it but..."

She looked at Davison, confused and said, "There was that huge monster that took Susan." Tears began to well in her eyes, and her voice wavered, "So what the fuck are these things, then? How many do we have to kill?"

"I have no idea," Davison said. "But they seem kind of…" He paused for a moment as he tried to put his thoughts into words. "I don't know...like a controlling device, but biological not mechanical. "

"It seems that way, doesn't it?" Perkins agreed, putting the wad of tissue back over his wound. "When you took that one from the German, he just collapsed, dead. "

"You think it's like mind control?" Beth said, glancing at both men.

"Something as near as dammit. But from what I saw on Hofner, he had no brain at all left. That animal took its place, the same with Jon."

"They are not like animals," Beth said as she closed her eyes for a moment, pushing down the pain in her body. "They must be more than that. Hofner could have left me to die out there, but he carried me into the airlock, to use me to get you to open the door."

"Don't worry about that," Davison said. "Them being intelligent or not doesn't change the fact that we have to kill them before they try to kill us." He pointed to the empty chains across the room, still hanging from the ceiling. "See them? Well, down in engineering there were chains too. People were hanging dead in them. The old crew. So they must have been here, too. Maybe the creature moved them? Who knows?"

"What does that have to do with anything?" Beth asked.

"Exactly! It means nothing. It has no bearing on why it does what it does. Or how it thinks. All that matters is that we find it. We kill it. End of story. So what if the little things aren't stupid. The big one? Who knows. We don't know which one knew enough about us to steal the spacesuits and air canisters from the airlock," Davison said.

"Or maybe it's just a coincidence," Beth said as she returned a weak smile. "*We* are the aliens here, remember." She then took a deep breath in before continuing, "Sure, Hofner said it was animals from all across the galaxy in some sort of collection, but we don't know that for sure. Not from him. These particular things could be native to Titan, they may want *us* gone from *their* home. Understandably."

"That's a very astute point," Perkins said aloud; the nicest thing he had ever said to Beth. He looked at Davison. "We may try to kill the big one, but then we have all the small ones as well. They—"

"Let's just concentrate on the one on the ship," Davison interjected.

"Okay." Perkins continued his train of thought. "*But* we never found Hofner's explosives, if there ever were any to begin with, which poses the question, what do we destroy that monster with? That is *if* we somehow manage to lure it."

"What about the armory?" Beth proffered.

"We'd have to go through engineering to get to that," Davison said.

"It's locked, and I tried to get in there. Besides, engineering was where we saw it last," Perkins added. "If we go there without a plan, we'd be walking into its trap. We really need to destroy it out in the open."

"Do you know if it's still down there?" Beth asked. "In engineering, I mean. "

"We last saw it there," Perkins reiterated.

"And we've mag-sealed the door and hatches on that level," Davison said.

"So we got no oxygen in our suits," Beth said. "And I don't have any tools to refill them from this ship's tanks. What then can we-"

"I know where you are going with this…" Davison cut in. "Whatever we decide to do, we have got to do it *inside* the ship. There's no running away from it."

"We have to kill it." Beth said.

"Do you have an idea where Bryce got to?" Perkins asked from the doorway.

"I never saw her." Beth said. "Maybe Hofner... I don't know. She just never came back. "

After a beat, Davison changed the subject back to the matter at hand, "So do you think we could kill that thing without leaving this ship?"

"It doesn't have to be an explosion. Electrocution is probably our best bet for safety. I may have an idea of how we *could* do it."

Davison pondered for a moment, before asking, "Does this ship have enough juice for something like that? We don't wanna use all the power and be stuck here."

"Are you kidding?" Beth said. "If I can hook the accelerators to the generators and pull the output filters off, we could fry half of this whole damn moon, and still fly home."

Suddenly, bright red lights flashed upon all of the consoles – an alarm, sounding much like an air raid siren.

It howled through the speakers.

"What the hell's that?" Davison asked.

Beth stood, the pain evident on her face, and made her way to a nearby console. She stared at the display. Though it was in German, she could decipher its red flashing graphics.

"It looks like a breach in life support," she said, examining the screen. "Pressure in engineering just dropped..."

"I guess that answers the question of where that thing is," Davison said with a grim smirk, before realizing gallows humor may not be the best thing in these circumstances.

"It opened a damn door?" Perkins said rhetorically above the sirens wail. He pointed to a high monitor that displayed a wireframe map of the ship's lower levels. A thick line flashed where the door to engineering had opened. "How the hell did it do that?"

The screen then flashed with another thick line, this time further down the corridor.

"It opened another," Beth said, astonished.

"This thing's getting smart, fast. It knows how to use our technology." Davison turned to Perkins. "Go into the security bay, we need eyes on it. Use the CCTV to see if you can keep track of it."

"Okay." Perkins sounded unsure. "But what are you both going to do? Beth's in no shape to fight this thing."

"We're gonna have to see if we can work out this electrocution idea," Davison replied, "and Beth's the only one who can do it, whatever shapes she's in."

"It's fine," she said, "I'll be okay. I'll just have to find some tools first, mine are out on Titan somewhere."

"I saw some in the next room, we'll have a look

there," Davison assured her. "You sure you're gonna be alright for this?"

"I'm gonna have to be." She quickly steadied herself against the console as a wave of dizziness hit her.

Behind a large monitor, surrounded by a dozen smaller screens, Perkins sat in a chair with his helmet on. He watched the video feeds displayed on the screens intently.

"Approaching corridor D now," came Davison's voice over his headset.

As he pressed a button on the console, the smaller monitors in front of him rotated their feeds. Each press of the button resulted in a new range of images from the ship's interior being displayed. The lights throughout the ship had since been turned on, and the dark ship was brightly lit.

Beth and Davison came into view on one of the feeds, both with their helmets on, walking slowly down a brightly lit corridor. Along the top of this video, the words *GANG D* were written in large digital white letters.

"I can see you," Perkins replied into his microphone as he pressed another button, sending that smaller image over to the main central monitor.

He watched as Davison moved ahead of Beth with his weapon held up, ready. Beth, unarmed, walked cautiously as she carried a small tool case in her hand.

"Any sign of our friend up there?" Davison asked.

Perkins scanned the smaller monitors, pressing the button to rotate the feeds.

"Nothing yet," he said. "Though I doubt it will be just strolling around. "

As he cycled the feed, one of the screens showed no

video, just static.

"One camera is out," Perkins continued. "I'm presuming it's the one in engineering. I can't see that room on any of the other screens."

As they moved further down the corridor, they soon disappeared off the main feed. Perkins switched the feed to another angle. He watched as they approached a part of the corridor where a few of the lights seemed to have burned out; they turned on the flashlights affixed to the front of their suits, casting out small thin beams into the shadows.

Coming to the familiar door marked '*Maschinenbau*', Davison paused, then glanced at Beth. "You ready?" he asked. "As I said before, there's quite a few bodies in here, including Jon and Wendy."

Nodding uncertainly, she looked at Davison through her helmet's visor, the blood from before now mostly wiped clean, though a redness still stained the metal grooves around its edges.

He removed the flashlight from his suit, then held it alongside the rifle barrel.

Perkins stared at the monitor feed. In the shadows of the corridor, he could only see the light from their flashlights.

"What shall I do?" he asked.

"Keep an eye out on all the screens you can," Davison replied. "Any movement, yell."

As the door to engineering slid open, Beth and Davison stared into the blackness beyond the entrance.

"Sorry, I couldn't get the lights on in here," Beth said

as the heat and smell in the room hit her, causing her to retch.

"Not your fault," Davison said under his breath as he looked in the room. From their vantage point, he could see the back of Jon's body lying in the same slumped position as before.

"Oh, no! Jon," Beth said, pained, as she fought her urge to vomit.

"Let's walk around him," Davison whispered. "We don't need to see that."

"Where's Wendy?"

"Don't worry. Just keep looking forward."

As they stepped quietly through the darkness, they gave Jon's corpse a wide berth.

"No offense Mike," Beth said under her breath, "but I wish Bryce was here instead of you."

"So do I," he replied, taking a deep breath in.

Beth followed close to his side, as he moved forward, his weapon aimed straight ahead.

Perkins had watched the flashlight beams disappear into the room; now he just stared at the other empty monitor feeds.

Engineering was as dark as it had been when Davison was last here. Their flashlights were dull and thin against the thickness of its oily shadows.

Gripping his light with one hand, he aimed it around the room; purposely avoiding where Jon and Susan's bodies still were.

In front of them, he had expected to see the group of bodies hanging from the ceiling, but his light only showed a collection of dangling chains, much like on the bridge, below which lay a few small chunks of unidentifiable meat.

"Looks like it's had its fill," Davison said quietly, as his light stayed on the scene. "Maybe if we're lucky, feeding time is over. "

Beth winced at not only the sight, but the smell that still lingered in her nose, the heat in the room making it much more revolting. Without any oxygen to their suits, their helmets gave them no respite from the fetid odor that permeated every crevice.

Still scanning the room with his rifle, Davison moved onward, past the chains. The flashlight in his hand threw its beam to where he pointed his weapon.

After inspecting any possible hiding places he could find, Davison felt momentarily secure. "I think it's gone from here," he said, still in a hush. "Anything there, Perkins?"

"Negative, Commander," Perkins said over the intercom.

"I need to go *there*," Beth said, pointing to an area of panels along the wall, next to what seemed like a large black container.

Nodding, Davison slowly walked to the lockers, looking around with his rifle ready. He may have felt more secure, but he was not so stupid as to assume that they were not still in constant danger. He would remain like this until the moment he could step back onto the parquet floor of his own house.

Crouching, Beth pulled a metal panel from out of the wall, then placed it softly onto the floor beside her. Exposing a glowing collection of wires and circuits beneath, she opened her toolbox as quietly as she could manage. Taking out a small handheld device, she connected its long cable to a motherboard within the open circuits. As she connected them, the screen on the device sprang to life. She looked at it intently, pressing buttons and flicking through menu screens.

"What are you thinking? Anything we can do?" Davison asked, not taking his eye off his aim around the room.

"I think I'm going to wire this into the busses above and below the corridor outside," Beth said as she worked.

"Will that do any damage to the ship?"

Shaking her head, she replied, "Nothing much. The insulation will be fried right off when we push this much current through it. "

"And us?" he replied. The more important question.

"As long as we're forward of the next bulkhead, we should be fine." Reaching into the panel, she began to work feverishly and at speed. Removing and reconfiguring wiring, inputting commands into the device. As she worked, she said, "Shouldn't be a problem routing this to the computer room," She then muttered under her breath, "Hopefully. "

Unseen by either of them, the large black container that stood only a few feet away silently dripped a slimy black fluid onto the floor around it.

The next few minutes passed by slowly for Davison. Each second felt like a minute. His focus never relented as he kept the rifle levelled at all times into the darkness of the room. He traced every part he could focus on, ensuring there was nothing lying in wait.

Every part, except one.

The large dark container against the wall next to them.

"What's that?" Beth whispered.

Pausing for a moment, Davison heard an intermittent clicking sound, and turned his aim to where the noise came from. The large black container. He stood in shock as it slowly unfolded itself into the form of the hideous creature. Each wall of this container was quickly exposed as one of the beast's black, armored, chitinous plates. The clicking sound grew louder as it reconfigured itself from the container into the monstrous form they had seen kill Susan.

Davison screamed, "Move!"

Pulling the device's cable from the exposed circuits, Beth then scrambled to get to her feet. The black slime that had dripped from this hidden beast had, though, already made it to where she had been crouched. As she scrambled, her foot slid out from underneath her and she fell to the floor.

The creature, now exposing its horrible flat-plated head with its jagged rows of teeth, roared loudly in defiance.

As he leveled his rifle, Davison saw in the light of his flashlight, the creature's chest. It parted like a large mouth. This grotesque maw opened up with terrifying speed. Then, not even a second later, one of the dark pulsating parasites fell from the opening and hit the floor with a squelch.

The small parasitic creature then squealed as it slithered at speed toward Beth, who scrambled in the slime beneath her, trying to stand up.

Perkins heard the commotion over the intercom.

He went pale as he listened to both Davison and Beth scream, along with the sound of gunfire.

Moving his aim away from the creature, Davison turned to the parasite and fired, stopping it in its tracks. The bullet hole in its body fizzed and sputtered black oil as it began to cave in on itself.

Grabbing Beth's arm, Davison dragged her to her feet, out of the path of the creature as it raised up fully and advanced on them.

Perkins, only hearing the creature's cacophony of predatory roars, had presumed the worst.

For those moments, he had despaired more than at any other time in his life.

"Run!" came Davison's cry over the intercom.

Perkins looked at the monitor hopefully.

The darkness of the on-screen corridor was broken when he saw Beth and the commander sprint from its shadows. With the device still in her hand, she led them away from the engineering room.

In an instant, Perkins got up from his seat and rushed out of the security room.

As Beth and the Commander ran at full speed down the long brightly lit corridor, they could hear the creature in pursuit clearly. They didn't have to glance back to know it was closing in on them fast.

As they approached the open bulkhead door at the end of the corridor, Davison slowed and motioned for Beth to go through first. Glancing over his shoulder, he saw the creature turn the corner a hundred or so feet away from them, its claws flailing in the air wildly as it approached at speed, smashing lights as it came.

Clearing the bulkhead, Beth saw Perkins standing outside the computer room door just ahead, his rifle in hand, aimed past her.

After running into the room, she immediately took the cable from the device in her hand and made her way to the room's main console. She plugged the cable into the socket below the built-in keyboard.

Moving past the bulkhead, Davison slammed on the button to close the door.

When nothing happened, he jabbed the button a few more times.

"Come on, come on," he muttered as the door slowly began to move.

The approaching creature's roar became more and more high-pitched. It clearly saw that its path through the bulkhead was narrowing.

In a panic, with only about a ten-inch gap left, Davison swung his rifle up at the creature, firing three times in a futile attempt to slow it down.

Perkins, meanwhile, shouted loudly to Beth from outside the computer room. "Do it now, Beth! Hurry!"

Before she could answer, the corridor echoed with a loud crash as the armored head of the creature slammed into the newly closed bulkhead door.

In a fury, again and again, it continued to hurl itself at the metal partition.

Through this door's small window, Davison stared at the creature, terrified.

"For God's sake Sladen... now!" Perkins cried into the room.

Beth frantically tried to work the terminal. "I can't find anything... All of this shit's in German!"

Punching more and more buttons on her device, the

main terminal suddenly changed its display to one that said:

Input/Output Language: English (US)

Relieved, Beth sighed, no longer handicapped by a language barrier.

Within Corridor D, beyond the safety of the bulkhead door, an explosion of electricity arced from the top of the corridor; a continuous streak of white and blue lightning that traced its way down to the floor, then worked its way back up again. As it consumed the corridor in its brightness, the electricity trapped the creature within its merciless power.

Davison shielded his eyes from the glare through the bulkhead door, as a horrible, high-pitched inhuman scream came from the creature's mouth. He watched as it was enveloped by the attacking electricity. After a while, its body shuddered, smoldered and began to burn from the inside out.

Beth backed away from the main terminal in the computer room as it began to spark. Smoke soon billowed out between the cracks of its panels.

Chapter Eleven
Detonation

The carcass of the creature, now a smoking mass, had been fused into the floor of Corridor D.

Perkins, Davison and Beth stood around with their helmets now clipped to their spacesuits' belts.

"Is it dead?" Perkins said, not moving his rifle's aim away from the blackened hulk.

Davison, crouched next to it, looked closely at the still mass for any sign of life. "I hope to every god up there that this is it," he replied.

"Did I do good?" Beth said, still with a relieved smile across her face.

Standing up, Davison put one hand on her shoulder, and replied with a smile. "Yes. But now? Now you just have to try to get this ship off this damn rock. "

With a nod, Beth said, "I'll go to engineering and get the rest of the power on. You guys go on ahead."

"You sure?" Davison asked. "What about Jon and Wendy?"

She nodded. "I'll be okay. I promise."

"Okay," Davison said, unconvinced, but knowing he should give her space. *Maybe she needed to see them to say goodbye?* "Well, we'll see you on the bridge when you're done," he said, and shrugged as he handed her his rifle. "Take this, in case any more of those little bastards are in here with us."

As Davison and Perkins made their way up to the top of the ship, Beth turned, the rifle slung over her shoulder. She looked down at the creature.

The corridor around her was partially lit from the creature's smashing of the bulbs. Her flashlight weakly shone onto its crumpled mass, reflecting on the black ooze that pooled out from around it.

As she gave the creature a light prod with her boot, she had half-expected it to lash out at her.

Walking up a small flight of stairs, Perkins stopped suddenly, looking worried. He'd heard something.

"What is it?" Davison asked.

"Shhhh!" Perkins said. He concentrated as he listened harder. After a moment of nothing, he went on, "It sounded like Sladen. "

Then, as if on cue, a monstrous roar carried down the corridors toward them.

They turned, horrified, back in the direction the noise had come from.

Beth hobbled down the corridor, tears streaming down her face. Her left hand cradled a large open wound on her side.

Behind her, the charred creature was rising to its feet, its flesh that had fused to the metal grate floor now ripping off its bulk. Around it, a previously hidden armored shell unfolded upward. As it did, it grew larger than it had been before. These newly exposed parts of the creature displayed none of the electrical burns that decorated the rest of it; instead they glistened healthily in the corridor's dim light.

"I thought it was dead," Davison said, as he stared down in horror at the now-vacant spot where the creature had been electrocuted. All that remained was a black residue slicked over the floor's metal grating, and small sections of charred, torn skin.

The weapon he gave to Beth now lay on the floor in front of him. He picked it up and held it tightly.

Perkins did not say a word. He felt like he was on an out-of-control rollercoaster, and there was nothing he could do to slow it down.

As Davison continued ahead of him down the corridor, Perkins briefly considered running back to the bridge and barricading the doors shut, leaving the rest of the crew to be eaten up by the impossibly unkillable alien.

With a throbbing agony in her side, Beth let out a low moan as she drifted in and out of consciousness. She felt chains wrap around her feet as her body was hoisted up, leaving her dangling upside down. As she swung, a trickle of blood dripped from her mouth, then ran over her skin down past her eye.

Perkins and Davison approached the closed door to engineering. Davison slowed his pace. He turned to Perkins, who followed a few feet behind, and whispered helplessly, "What do we do?"

Perkins looked into Davison's wide eyes, and realized then that Beth was not just a member of the crew to this man. Davison obviously *loved* her. And this love seemed to have rendered him weak.

Before Perkins could think of a platitude to appease Davison's panic, his gaze drifted toward the closed door;

to something at the window, something caught by the beam from his flashlight.

Perkins' face turned white as the color drained from his cheeks. "Jesus in heaven," he said as a cold fear crept over him.

Davison turned slowly to the window, where his eyes locked with the creature. The monster stared at them through the glass, its shark-like eyes blinking vertically. Emotionless.

Backing away, careful not to break eye contact with this beast, Perkins spoke quietly to Davison. "If you want in there, I think I'll be able to find another way."

Davison's eyes darted to Perkins, before returning to the creature. "What? How?"

"All these ships follow the same layout. All engineering rooms must have direct access to the cargo bay, in order for direct atmospheric purging, in case of fire or gas. It's a health and safety standard. Usually installed as service hatches. Same for the Germans as it is for us. So I can go find it. Then we can lure that *thing* out and save Beth."

Twenty feet further up the corridor from engineering, Davison had his back up against the wall. With his helmet back on, he was now cloaked in a thick shadow, his rifle aimed in the direction of the closed room.

The only sound he could hear was his own terrified breathing.

His thoughts raced. *If it can override mag-locked doors, why in the hell didn't it do so at the bulkhead? Was it taunting us? Knowing we couldn't do a thing to hurt it?*

"Davison?" Perkins said quietly over the intercom.

"You find anything?" Davison asked.

"I'm in a corridor leading to the cargo bay. I should be there in the next minute. Do you think Ms. Sladen is okay? Have you heard anything?"

Davison ignored his sinking feeling. "I hope she's okay. Haven't heard a thing. "

"Okay, let me know if anything changes. "

Outside the ship, the storm had passed, leaving the SMS Frerichs in a heavy veil of shadow.

A figure stood on the surface, glancing up at the ship from the safety of the darkness. To them the ship looked like a metal corpse, bereft of any life.

In the distance, a faint rumble of thunder echoed from outside of the crater, threatening to break in.

Winding his way through a narrow corridor of pipes, valves and crates, Perkins trod as silently as he could until he arrived at a door.

Opening it, he then stepped into the cargo bay; an imposing room with crates lining the walls, and a large metal cargo net suspended from the ceiling. The lights in here – like the other lower levels of the ship – were dull from running on reduced power. Yet as there were more bulbs in the bay, the room appeared much brighter than the corridors.

At one end of the bay, he spotted the body hanging from a locker; the one Bryce had found upon their first visit. Ignoring its dead-eyed stare, he glanced around the rest of the area.

Perkins was not being selfless in this mission. He was only thinking of himself. It just so happened that this was something that also cast him – for once – in a favorable light.

Without Beth, he and Davison could not escape in this ship; it was as simple as that. Maybe Davison could have flown the Shenandoah solo, but this was a totally different vessel. She *had* to be saved in order for them to survive.

As to why he was the one who'd volunteered to go save her? The answer was even simpler. He would rather sneak behind enemy lines than face that creature head on.

As he walked cautiously by a pile of wooden crates, his eyes darted to the label on them that said *'Achtung: Zündstoff'*. He did not need a translation for this; underneath those words was the icon of an explosion.

"I think I found something..." Perkins said to Davison, who was still waiting in the shadows. "Seems I may owe Hofner an apology, because I'm standing right in front of a crate of explosives."

Davison's eyes widened.

"I had a look inside. Each has six aluminum cylinders in them," Perkins continued.

Quietly, Davison said, "Sounds like excavation ammunition. Is anything written on them?"

"They say Alpha One Six, E.S., Made in England."

"And how many crates are there?" Davison asked.

"Ten."

"Wow," Davison said, "They aren't taking chances. That's enough to blow apart half of this moon."

After a long pause, Perkins spoke hesitantly. "I think I may have a way to dump that thing outside and blast him to kingdom come. Can you wait a while longer?"

"Why?"

"We're going to have to lure it down there. I have some preparing to do."

He pushed a lever on the wall of the cargo bay, and Perkins cowered as the mechanics above him clanked and screeched loudly to life.

Glancing around fearfully, he hoped that the monster in the ship would not be alerted by this noise.

"I'm at the door," Davison whispered to him over the intercom. "I can't see it, but I think you're clear. I couldn't hear anything you're doing from up here."

As the metal net descended from above, Perkins scanned the wall around him, looking for the service hatch to engineering.

He saw a sign up on the wall saying *'Maschinenbau'*, and recognized it from the door on the level above. *'Engineering.'*

Crossing the cargo bay, he glanced at the explosive from the crate he had clipped onto his belt. Despite the room being as hot as it was in engineering, his sweat was more due to the fear. He was getting in over his head, he thought. But at least everything was going to plan. So far.

The hatch ahead was obscured from view by several large pieces of machinery. He circumnavigated them by climbing over some boxes, and his mouth dropped.

"Oh shit," he said under his breath.

"What is it? What's the matter?" Davison said over the intercom.

Perkins did not reply.

"Perkins, do you read me?"

With every one of his senses on edge, Perkins moved silently backward, climbing back over the boxes, then he turned and bolted toward the cargo bay doors.

"Perkins?" Davison called into the helmet

microphone.

He was left with no choice.

"Fuck it," he said through gritted teeth.

Raising his gun, he hit the door-release with his hand.

Nothing.

Furrowing his brow, he hit the button again.

Nothing.

Again.

Nothing.

Turning his gun toward the controls, he fired a single shot.

Perkins looked wildly around the cargo bay as he unclipped the bomb from his belt. The red LED display illuminated as he pressed the buttons. Frantically he scrolled through the menu system.

>DETONATE
>ARM
>TIMER
>DELAY

He pressed the return key, then cycled through the next options.

>20min
>10min
>5min

He pressed the return key again.

>CONFIRM TO ARM

Swallowing hard, he pressed the return key once more.

As he looked down at the next blinking screen, a bead of sweat dropped from his forehead into the glass of his visor.

>CONFIRM TO COMMENCE DELAY

He closed his eyes, and prayed to his chosen god – NTI – for strength.

Behind him, a large dark mass rose up from the darkness, casting a shadow over him.

Opening his eyes again, Perkins saw it - the looming shadow standing over him at his back. Slowly, and against his better judgement, he turned around.

Then, for the second time on this mission, he lost control of his bladder.

As he cowered, tears filling his eyes, he caught sight of the level for the large net.

Beth hung unconscious from the ceiling, still drifting in and out of consciousness.

Not fully aware of her surroundings, she caught glimpses of the door to the corridor in front of her, where the light beyond it glowed dimly.

Then blackness.

She then saw a glimpse of Davison trying to open those sliding doors with his hands.

Then blackness.

Next she saw him squeezing through the small gap he had pushed open, his rifle then held at the ready as he scanned the surroundings.

Blackness.

She saw him run toward her.

Blackness.

She came to once more as Davison lifted her down onto the floor. As he unwrapped the chains from her ankles, he looked into her half-open eyes and said, "It's okay, Beth. I don't think it's here anymore. You're safe. "

Blackness.

Her last moment of clarity was of hearing Perkins shouting over the speaker in Davison's helmet. He sounded in pain as he said between screams, "HELP ME, MICHAEL! PLEAAAAAASE"

The sound of his screams soon dissipated as the blackness took a greater hold of her.

Scanning the engineering room with his flashlight, Davison soon spotted a service hatch at the other end of the room. Speedily navigating his way there, he pushed it open.

Inside, a wide circular room stretched itself downward into the unwelcoming darkness. A wide ladder affixed to the nearest wall beckoned him down.

"PLLEEEEEEAASEEE. HEEEELLLLLPP." Perkins' screams continued over his intercom.

Unable to endure the cries anymore, Davison removed his helmet, threw it to the floor and stared down into the hatch.

He had no choice.

He had to help.

He had to descend.

In her dreams, Beth stood naked in front of Davison. She leaned forward and kissed him.

This was the way many of her happy dreams started, but the romance of the moment soon shifted to horror, as his expression changed and he wrapped his hands around her throat with a murderous glint in his eyes.

Opening his mouth, what came out of it was not his own voice, but the same monstrous roar the creature had made.

His teeth then started to simultaneously drop out from his gums, ripped out from their beds then replaced by razor-sharp, serrated incisors.

The nightmare seemed to reach its peak, but then her subconscious amped up the horror even more. As Davison throttled the life from her, she gasped her last breaths. Then he leaned into her, roaring loudly in her face, as his eyes burst outward. Their jelly exploded from his sockets and splattered over her face – into her open mouth. Within this dream, her life was extinguished by the man she loved, as his two empty eyes were replaced by two onyx-colored orbs.

Inside the cargo bay, Davison crouched behind a large pile of metal and wooden crates. With the hatch now closed behind him, he steeled himself as the whimpers of the NTI representative hung heavily in the air. Like a wounded animal close to its demise, Perkins' high-pitched cries were both terrifying and heart-breaking.

As silently as he could, Davison moved his way to the edge of the crates; paused for a moment, then – summoning all of his bravery – peered around the corner.

Tangled within the suspended cargo net, Perkins and the creature were entwined; trapped together within its metal confines.

Blood poured out from Perkins' nose as the creature,

from behind, chewed slowly on the side of his neck, its teeth digging in deep.

Perkins' eyes slowly opened and fixed on Davison. His arm wagged slowly through the netting, motioning weakly to the main cargo bay doors.

"Davisssssoon. Opeeeeennn," he gargled. As he slowly drowned in his own blood, his waving arm stopped, and his life slowly ebbed away.

Davison's eyes wandered helplessly from this execution to the cargo bay door, then back again.

He then saw what Perkins' not only held in his hand.

As the creature tore through his neck, Perkins half-smiled, then pressed the button on the bomb that he gripped in his hand.

The creature, though, remained oblivious and continued to feast on him.

It didn't notice or care when its prey died. It just continued to rip at Perkins' flesh with its teeth, tearing large chunks off as it carried on chewing loudly.

Focusing on Perkins' tightly gripped hand, Davison saw the bomb was active, as its screen flashed red numbers in a countdown.

The timer had begun.

5:00...

4:59...

4:58…

Without another thought for his safety, nor with any time to mourn the loss of Perkins, Davison leapt out from his hiding place and sprinted over to the side of the bay doors.

As he slammed his gloved hand through the small frame of glass on the wall, he pressed the emergency release button sitting below it.

Without thinking of his own safety, he stood frozen as a loud siren rang out. Soon the deafening wail was accompanied by the noise of the outside coming in. Blasts of freezing, toxic air, rushing in like a gale from the opening that appeared around the lowering bay doors.

As Titan's elements were introduced to the inside of the ship, the change in atmosphere began to suck everything not bolted down in the cargo bay, out to the moon's surface.

Fighting the clawing winds, Davison managed to hit the net's release lever.

After this, Davison was unable to fight the elements anymore, and he was dragged outside to the awaiting Forseti crater.

Slamming into the moon's surface, Davison immediately began coughing and gagging from not only breathing the poisonous atmosphere, but also from the blasts of dirt that blew into his lungs. Climbing to his feet, he staggered back up the still-open ramp, trying to hold his breath as much as he could.

He glanced back and heard the creature's roar. Behind him the net had been dragged out as well, and now the beast fought to free itself.

Beth's eyes slowly opened, the throbbing in her side dragging her out of her nightmare. Her eyes darted about the room, afraid the creature would be still watching her.

Wait, she thought. *Was Davison here? Did I imagine it? No. He freed me.*

Sitting up, she winced in pain and gripped her side. The wound, though still seeping blood, had a cloth pressed firmly into it.

Before she had time to ponder any more of what

happened, the service hatch door at the back of the room burst open. Gusts of Titan's wind blew out from within, causing everything in the room to vibrate.

As Davison fell through the hatch, the wind blew its inward opening door shut, keeping the violent atmosphere trapped.

Crawling to her feet, Beth moved over to Davison, who now lay with his back on the floor, gasping for air. From his brief time outside the cargo bay, his skin already showed the same signs of frostbite that hers had.

"What happened?" she said as she fell down to her knees beside him. The pain in her side made her grit her teeth.

Gasping for air, Davison took no more time to recover as he dragged himself to his feet. "We gotta get to the bridge," he wheezed.

They staggered as fast as they could down Corridor D.

Davison held onto Beth, one of her arms over his shoulder. He was more than just helping her; they were steadying each other's journey. Both of their bodies felt pain. Both suffered the effects from their recent outside exposure, but Beth also had open wounds from the creature to contend with.

As they turned a corner, they got to one of the bulkhead doors.

Frantically pressing the button to open it, they were soon met on the other side by a torrent of Titan's wind. With the bulkhead door open, the corridor to the bridge stretched out in front of them.

Standing in their path: the creature.

Behind it, the inner airlock door had been smashed

inward, the outer door having been torn from its hinges.

Roaring, this creature advanced toward them, portions of the cargo net still wrapped around its body.

Behind it, some netting remained trailing onto the ground. Caught in this wake, only a few inches from the creature's back, the remnants of Perkins could be seen, the bomb still gripped in his hand.

From outside, the relentless winds of Titan blasted toward them, as the countdown on the bomb flashed wildly.

32...

31...

30...

Before Davison could react, and with the wind already dragging him and Beth forward, the creature lunged at him.

As the atmosphere stole the oxygen from their lungs, the creature stole Davison from Beth's arms.

Thrown out of the now ripped open airlock, Davison smashed onto the dirt floor. Clawing at his throat again, trying to breathe, he tried to fight through the suffocation and pain.

As the fumes and piercing cold attacked his body, he had no time to think.

The creature soon followed him out of the airlock and stood over him.

With one of its large claws, it grabbed one of Davison's feet, then lifted him up from the ground. After it stood up to its full height, it held him at an upside-down eye-level.

Choking, Davison saw the creature's mouth salivating in a grin. He could see that this was no mere mindless beast; this was personal for the creture. It was toying with him, and enjoying every moment.

Looking down, Davison saw the display on the bomb at the end of its countdown.

5...
4...
3...

Closing his eyes, with his lungs on fire, Davison tried to picture Beth's face.

2...
1...

Nothing.

Wheezing out the last of his oxygen, as the creature dangled him playfully, he glanced down at the bomb's display screen.

MALFUNCTION

The creature studied Davison's contorting face as his body writhed to break free, slowly losing his life. Soon, the man in the creature's grip stopped moving, unconsciousness stealing him away as the oxygen in his lungs ran out.

The creature tossed Davison aside as if he weighed nothing, then looked up to the skies above Titan and roared.

Beth had made it to the bridge, her body almost void of strength.

She did not know if it was possible to feel more pain than she felt right now.

As she made her way to the observation window, she looked down at the scene below.

She watched as the creature threw Davison aside and roared. She could not help but scream.

On the surface, the creature turned toward the ship, ready to hunt the other human.

The creature's path to the airlock, though, was no longer clear.

In an NTI spacesuit, a lone figure stood in its way. This figure had a collection of air canisters hooked around its belt, and in their hands, a large rifle.

"Not your day, is it?" Bryce said as she took aim at the bomb, still caught in the beast's netting.

Before the creature could mount an attack, she steadied her stance and fired.

From the bridge window, Beth watched as a tremendous explosion rocked the surface outside. The blast ripped the creature apart as the ground beneath it began to crack and give way.

As the dirt crumbled beneath it, a sinkhole opened, dragging the creature's remains into the darkness below.

Davison came to, his head throbbed wildly; the pain was almost blinding him. Through the agony, he managed to focus on Beth and Bryce both talking to each other, sitting on the seats next to him. They were in the medical bay.

"Of course it malfunctioned!" Beth was saying to Bryce. "There's a reason NTI doesn't use those things! Now if it was American made… That's another story."

Bryce laughed. "We'd probably all be dead if that was the case."

With a cracked voice, Davison managed to break into their conversation, "I thought I died..."

Beth turned, excited. "You're awake! How are you feeling, El Comandant?"

"I'm fine," he said, wheezing. "What about those other things, the parasites?"

Bryce replied, "We searched the ship from head to toe. Sealed off all exposed areas and only found the remains of about three of them."

Beth shrugged. "My guess is they all died when the creature did. All part of the same life. Like a hive mind."

For a moment, Davison turned from Beth to look at Bryce curiously.

"I know," she said pre-empting his questions, "I couldn't have timed it better."

"Where *were* you?" he asked, as he tried to cough the pain out.

"I hid out after I escaped from Hofner," Bryce explained. "Waited for a while for him to leave, then went back to the Shenandoah when I thought it would be safe. But no one was there. So I came here."

"You were gone a *long* time," he noted with an air of suspicion as he looked into her eyes.

After a long beat and a look of apology, she replied, "... I... I got lost."

Her face told Davison that not only was it a painful admission, but it was embarrassing as well.

A trace of a smile appeared on his face. Beth grabbed Davison by the hand and asked, "Are we having fun yet?"

With a pained smile, he replied, "All I know is, I need a *damned* coffee."

Epilogue

The moon of Titan had, over the millennia, endured myriad hardships as it lay within the shadow of its parental gas giant; from meteor showers to cataclysmic shifts within its own core, it somehow endured everything it had faced. And now, as the thrusters from the SMS Frerichs lifted it off this moon's surface, Titan had done what it had done best. It had endured again.

Not that anything of note had happened. This moon had witnessed parasites invading its confines many, many times before. Different parasites over different eras, each hailing from various rocks within the confines of the known and unknown universes. Each one of them had taken their turns infecting its surface, causing their own minute damage. Then, after a while, they would always leave. Whether from expiration or by leaving voluntarily. In the end, they never stayed long.

As for this latest parasitic colonizer, as with every one that came before it, it had passed without fanfare. These new parasites had gone, never to return again.

Of course, at some point in time, *other* parasites would arrive. And then, just like every other time, Titan would sit, watching and waiting patiently, until their insignificant actions would come quietly to an end.

Printed in Great Britain
by Amazon